A T_____
WITHOUT
A NAME

PENELOPE S. DELTA

A TALE
WITHOUT
A NAME

Translated and illustrated by
Mika Provata-Carlone

PUSHKIN PRESS
LONDON

English translation © Mika Provata 2013

A Tale Without a Name first published as
Paramythi horis onoma in 1911

This edition first published in 2013 by
Pushkin Press
71–75 Shelton Street,
London WC2H 9JQ

ISBN 978 1 908968 90 6

Illustrations © Mika Provata 2013

Set in 10 on 13 Monotype Baskerville
by Tetragon, London

and printed in Great Britain on Munken Premium White 90 gsm
by TJ International Ltd, Padstow, Cornwall

www.pushkinpress.com

A TALE
WITHOUT
A NAME

I

The Forest

W HEN OLD KING PRUDENTIUS realized that he had little time left to live, he summoned his son, young Witless, and said to him:

"You've had your fill of frolics and amusements for long enough, my son. The time has come for you to marry, and to take in your hands the governance of the State. My time is over. It is now your turn to rule well and to be a good king."

He therefore dispatched his High Chancellor to the neighbouring kingdom to seek the hand of the beautiful Princess Barmy, on behalf of Witless, son of Prudentius I, King of the Fatalists.

The wedding took place amidst great joy and sumptuous feasting, and a few days later, after he had given his blessing to his children, old Prudentius went the way of all flesh, and Witless was crowned king.

Everything seemed rosy and enviable for the young couple. The coffers of old Prudentius were filled to bursting point with gold florins; the kingdom was ringed and strong-walled by mighty citadels brimming with soldiers; the splendid palace, built high up on a densely wooded mountain, reigned supreme over the capital below, where its citizens lived in good prosperity; wide and well-paved thoroughfares linked the kingdom of the Fatalists with kingdoms nearby.

Everywhere one looked there was joy and good life.

And in whichever direction the new king might turn his eye, looking out from the high donjon tower of his palace, he could see endless sown fields, gorges and vales bursting with the lushest vegetation, cities and villages with neat and pretty dwellings, mountains thick with woods, and pastures of the greenest green. There were countless cows grazing in happy company with flocks of sheep and goats. And the farmers labouring the land were as busy and as numerous as ants, milking the cows, shearing the sheep, transporting grain and produce to the capital, where they would sell them.

Many years passed.

Time, which turned to white Witless's hair, and caused it to moult, Time, which withered the fair beauty of Queen Barmy, also transformed the entire aspect of the kingdom of the Fatalists.

Everywhere was wasteland. Endless dales, barren and untilled, stretched to the farthest corners of the kingdom, and only some few, dilapidated ruins bore witness to the places where in the olden times there had stood proud and fearsome the formidable citadels of Prudentius I.

Here and there, a miserable, ramshackle hovel broke the monotony of the deserted valley. Weeds and rubble covered the hills; the neglected roads vanished beneath the thorn bushes that spread unchecked their spiny, tangled twigs in every direction.

Whistling shrilly among the rubble and the rocks, the wind bewailed the desolation of the land.

The great woods alone remained in their place, forgotten, unlaboured, concealing under their burgeoning foliage an entire universe of butterflies, beetles, weevils and bees, which enjoyed undisturbed the sweet-scented wild flowers. There were great hosts of wild strawberry plants, blossoming and bearing fruit in brotherly company with the brambles, their fruit rotting and dropping useless on the ground.

The footpaths, which in the olden days had led through the trees, these too had been long erased, for long had it been since the time when a human foot had walked on them. And the trees, the shrubs and the undergrowth had so forgotten what a human form looked like that they were all shocked and startled, they shivered and trembled, and murmured frightened whispers to one another when, one day, they saw a young boy, with dusky, dream-laden brown eyes, walking under their foliage, stopping at every step in order to look here at a flower, there at an insect, with amazement and surprise, as though he were seeing them for the very first time.

"Hark, what sort of thing is this that walks past?" asked a lentisk fearfully, drawing back its leaves, scared that the boy might see it.

"Who knows!" replied the pine. "Perhaps it could be a different kind of deer?"

A poplar, standing erect nearby, tilted its proud head ever so slightly to catch a glimpse of the passer-by.

"A deer?" it said in a burst of laughter, which caused all of its leaves to turn upside down, so that in an instant its colour changed from fresh green to shimmering silver. "You must be dreaming, my lad! A deer has four legs and this one only has two!"

"Well, what sort of animal is it then?" asked a bramble anxiously. "Could it be wicked? Will it eat up my new suit of clothes, so that summer should find me naked?"

"Do not torment your little heads, my children," said the old plane tree, "for this is no animal, nor does it graze on leaves. It has been many years since one of them passed this way. Yet I remember that there was a time when our forest was teeming with others like him. Those were the good times, when people gathered the honey of the bees, and the strawberries of the strawberry shrub, the blackberries, and the ripe, fire-golden fruit of the arbutus tree."

"What's that?" exclaimed the wild strawberry, huddling close at the feet of the old plane tree. "What are you saying, grandfather? Could this be… *a man?*"

"Yes, most certainly indeed, *it is a man*," replied the old plane tree.

And the poplar muttered:

"But yes, of course, that's what it is, a man! I remember now having seen others like him in my youth."

The lentisk spread out its branches with vivid curiosity, so as to get a closer look at him.

"A man?" asked the haughty oak. "And what does he want in our realm, might I ask?"

And all the trees leant forward, to see the "man", as he passed by.

He was a slender boy, no more than sixteen years old. His velvet clothes, woven with gold and silver, were now threadbare at the elbows and the knees and far too small for him, rugged and torn; the golden ribbons that held his sandals to his feet were all ripped and frayed, secured into place with clumsy, knobbly knots.

He lay down at the roots of the old plane tree, saw the wild strawberry shrub by his side, heavy with red-ripe fruit; he picked the berries and ate them. Then he folded his arms under his head to make a pillow, and fell asleep.

He slept such a deep sleep that he did not hear the whisperings of the trees, nor the gurgling of the brook which flowed nearby, nor even yet the whistling of the blackbird, which, hopping from branch to bough, was telling the most extraordinary tales.

"The King's son!" exclaimed the old plane tree. "How can I possibly believe this, when I look at his bare legs and tattered clothes?"

"And yet believe it you must!" replied the blackbird with a caw. "Heed my words, I fly in and out of the palace windows, I know all that goes on in there."

"But why doesn't he change his clothes?" asked the pine, thoroughly appalled.

"Because he has no other clothes, of course!" came the blackbird's reply.

"What's that? The King's son?" exclaimed the thyme, offering up its budding flowers to the buzzing bee, who was seeking a place to land and suck their honey.

"Hah! You seem surprised!" came the shrill skirling of the blackbird. "Perhaps you think that the King himself has greater riches than a humble shepherd or a bargeman?"

"What you are saying is strange indeed!" murmured the lentisk, who would not allow himself to be convinced.

"And yet believe him you must," said the bee, fluttering around him. "He is telling the truth. The King himself wears clothes just like these. And if you only saw the princesses, then you would be truly horrified!"

"Why?" enquired the strawberry shrub.

The blackbird leapt by its side, and whispered:

"*Because underneath their robes, they do not even have a shirt on!*"

And he burst into laughter, not realizing that he was standing right by the boy's ear.

The Prince woke up with a jump, startled out of his sleep.

The blackbird took fright and flew away, the bee hid among the leaves of the lentisk, while the trees lifted up their heads, feigning indifference, as though they had neither seen nor heard a single thing.

Dusk had fallen. The Prince got up and started again on his way. He came out of the forest, crossed the arid, waterless vale, and, turning towards the palace with a quick step, went up the mountain, clambering up the rocks and dry earth as nimbly as a young kid goat.

II

Court and Courtiers

FROM THE GREAT and splendid royal fortress of Prudentius I, only the high donjon tower was now habitable. Everything else—the great halls, the parapet walks, the barracks—all had crumbled to rubble. The tower itself was in a most derelict state. No one ever took care to repair the collapsing plaster. And the wind roamed and wandered unhindered, whistling shrilly in the empty chambers, where most of the windows were now left bereft of their glazing.

The thick walls, however, held strong still. And it was there, in a small number of rooms, that the King and his family had to confine themselves.

As he approached the palace, the Prince could hear angry voices, female as well as male.

He halted for a moment. Then, with a heavy sigh, he made as though to turn and go away again. Yet at that very moment a girl, fifteen or so, leapt out of the rubble and threw herself at his neck.

"Oh, sweet brother, at last you have returned!" she said to him with tears in her eyes. "If only you knew how long I have been waiting for you!"

The Prince kissed her and asked her sadly:

"What is all this screaming again?"

"What do you suppose it is? The same, always the same! Spitefulnia is squabbling with Jealousia, and father, in his efforts to separate them, is only fuelling their anger."

"And what is mother doing?"

"What would you expect? She is busy making herself pretty, as ever!"

"And you, my Little Irene?"

"I... I..." She hid her face in her hands and burst into tears. "*I* came out to find you, because you are the only one who knows how to soothe and to offer comfort."

He sat on the flat stone next to her and rested his chin on the palm of his hand, pensive, listening to the screaming which still persisted in the palace.

Little Irene threw her arm around his neck.

"Say something to me, please do," she begged fondly.

"What shall I say?" muttered her brother. "I am going to go away, Little Irene."

"You'll go away? Where will you go?"

"Where every man who wishes to live with dignity goes, where all those who have left our kingdom and forsaken their country have gone."

"And you would leave me behind?"

The Prince kissed her.

"No, my Little Irene. I shall take you with me."

"Irene! Little Irene!" boomed a voice from behind the walls. "Little Irene, where are you? Come along, then, and bring us your smile. I am tired of your older sisters and their screaming!"

At that, the King, his crown askew on his bald head, his mantle worn to shreds, appeared in the doorway.

Brother and sister got up and followed their father to the room where all the family had gathered.

Before a cracked mirror stood Queen Barmy. Two maids were braiding flowers and old, discoloured ribbons through her silvery-white hair, while with their backs turned to one another, at the two opposite ends of the room, sat the two elder princesses, long-faced, with pursed lips, cross and ill-tempered.

"Hark at the beauty and familial joy," said the King, crossing his arms, and looking in turn at Jealousia and Spitefulnia. "This is how we pass the day, every day: one of the two yells white, while the other one howls black!"

"This is nothing compared to what *I* have to suffer, poor miserable me!" bemoaned Queen Barmy. "You only have your two daughters to complain about. What about me, having to cope with you, deafening me with your screams, and with your precious son, going off wandering just when I need him to go and fetch me pretty little flowers…"

Yet, seeing that her tears were causing her nose to redden, she stopped abruptly, smiled to her mirror, and with solemn gravity concentrated on attaching to her belt a great tin star.

The King stood up and rang the bell to summon one of his servants. Yet no one came. He rang again, and still no one appeared.

This made him exceedingly cross; he went to the doorway, and began to stamp his feet on the ground, shouting angrily:

"To the devil with all of you! You call yourselves my servants! I will have everyone's head off!"

At this, frightened and panting, came the High Chancellor. A tin chain jingled around his neck.

"My lord, please, forgive your unworthy slave—" he began.

"Where are all those monkey-faced servants of mine?" interrupted the King irritably. "Why is there no response when I ring the bell?"

Then, seeing the chain, he burst all of a sudden into a guffaw.

"What's that you have slung around your neck instead of your golden chain of state?" he asked.

The High Chancellor grew red in the face, mumbled, his words became confused; he froze with embarrassment, and fell silent.

"What's that you are saying?" exclaimed the King. "You sold it? And what for?"

"So that Your Majesty could dine yesterday," replied the High Chancellor in an almost inaudible murmur, bowing low all the way to the ground.

"Ah!... Hmm!... So be it," said the King. "I forgive you this time."

He wrapped himself majestically in the tatters of his mantle and continued:

"Give the orders for the Cellar Master to come. My throat is parched, and I desire to sweeten it with amber-coloured wine from the islands, such as even the King my Royal Uncle would envy! And then command the Master of the Household to set the table. Why does he keep us waiting? The hour is late."

Bent double, almost to the ground, the High Chancellor stood perfectly still, not moving a muscle.

"Well, did you not hear me?" said the King, raising his royal head even higher. "What are you waiting for?"

"Your Majesty… your Cellar Master has gone, and the cellar is empty."

"What are you saying?" bellowed the King.

"What are you saying?" echoed Spitefulnia.

And forgetting both tantrums and mulishness, seized by the greater fear of hunger, she leapt up from her seat, while the maids dropped the Queen's hair, and anxiously they too approached to listen.

The High Chancellor bowed ever so slightly lower, yet made no reply.

The King scratched his bald head nervously, and his crown now slid gloomily over to his left ear.

Somewhat numbed, he asked:

"Is there *no* food?"

The High Chancellor, still bowing low, offered up for display the open palms of his two hands, showing the King that they were empty.

His Majesty understood. He abandoned his imperious tone, together with the gold-embroidered mantle, which now hung trailing behind him, deplorable and pitiful in its ragged state.

He marched once or twice around the room, then sat on a lame, hole-ridden armchair; and, sending his crown with one determined shove from left to right ear, he made a decision:

"Cunningson, come here!"

The High Chancellor straightened his back, and advanced towards the King.

"My liege…" he said, bowing once more.

"What would you advise?" the King asked curtly.

The High Chancellor fixed his eyes silently upon his royal master's crown, which glittered with a goodish few precious and sizeable stones encrusted in the golden frame.

The King understood the meaning of the gaze, and aghast seized his crown with his two hands, holding it secure upon his head.

"Oh, no! Never that!" he shouted nervously. "Advise again."

"Well, then, and since the equerries whom I sent to the neighbouring kingdoms some ten days ago have not returned, may His Royal Highness the Prince go once more to the King your Royal Cousin…"

"No," said the Prince firmly, coming out of the corner where he and Little Irene had withdrawn. "I took an oath never to beg again."

The King sprang to his feet and stood straight and erect before his son, menacing him with his fist.

"And who are you, you little imp, to have taken oaths, and to have opinions?" he said crossly.

"I am the future king," replied his son quietly, "and I wish to preserve my dignity."

Witless rubbed his forehead with furious rage. He could find no answer to give to his boy, and yet the problem remained unresolved: where were they to find food?

"Cunningson!" he finally shouted frantically. "Either you find me a solution, or I shall have your head cut off!"

The miserable Cunningson was most profoundly distressed. He began to tremble and to shake in earnest, and he kept glancing at the door, gauging with his eye how many steps he would have to take in order to reach it.

"Well, then, out with it! A solution!" yelled the King.

The High Chancellor was quivering all over.

"I… I ought to go myself, then…" he suggested, his voice a mere whisper.

"Well then, go, and see that you run!" replied the King. "I want food and wine, at once. If you do not leave and come back as quick as lightning, I shall have your head cut off!"

Before he had even finished his phrase, the High Chancellor was already far away.

Cunningson bolted out of the palace as fast as he could. Yet once outside in the darkness and the cold, he stopped still.

"Where am I going?" he muttered. "And how? It would take me two days to reach the realm of the King the Royal Cousin, and till then…"

For two long minutes he stood there, considering the situation. Then he made up his mind.

"Today, tomorrow, what difference does it make!" he mumbled. "I am going away in any case! I just need to wrap up some unfinished business first, with my friend Faintheart…"

He began to scramble down the mountain.

As he was hurrying down, he heard footsteps nearby. A cold shiver ran through him.

"Who's that?" he asked, petrified.

"No one, Your Excellency, it is only I!" answered a voice, even more petrified than his own.

The High Chancellor found his lost courage once more. "And *who* might *you* be?" he asked.

"It… It is I… Miserlix the blacksmith," answered the quivering voice.

"Show yourself here before me at once!" commanded the High Chancellor.

And a human shadow, with a heavy bulge over its shoulder, appeared in front of him.

The High Chancellor seized the bulge.

"You thieving rogue! What have you got in your haversack?" he demanded savagely.

"Your Excellency… I am no rogue and no thief… These are my chickens, and my wine, which I have bought and paid for—"

"You lie!" barked the High Chancellor more brutally still. "Ragged beggars such as yourself eat no chickens and drink no wine! You have stolen these goods! Tell me now where from!"

"I have not stolen them, master, peace be with you, I paid for these!" answered Miserlix, his voice breaking into sobs. "I paid for these, master, I did, with the money I got selling my daughter's needlework, a commission from the King the Royal Uncle, the sovereign of the kingdom across the border. Ask Him, Your Excellency, if I paid or not! He even gave me a gift, a shepherd's pie…"

He was given, however, no chance to finish what he was saying. Cunningson was not likely to miss out on such an incredible stroke of good luck.

He snatched the haversack from Miserlix, who stood frozen, transfixed with terror, and with a sharp kick sent him rolling down the slope so viciously and violently that the poor man did not regain his foothold until he had reached the foot of the high mountain.

III

At the Humble Cottage of Mistress Wise

C UNNINGSON SCURRIED in all haste back to the palace and entered the room where the King, the Queen, the princesses and the maids-in-waiting all sat in a circle, watching amidst great fits of laughter the buffooneries of a podgy, hunchbacked and knock-kneed fool.

By the window stood the Prince, who was talking to Little Irene, describing to her the beauties of the woods where he had been that afternoon.

Their talk was disrupted by the screams with which everyone else in the room greeted Cunningson's entrance; the two siblings turned around, bewildered.

The High Chancellor opened his haversack with great pomp and circumstance, and presented its contents—two roast chickens, three bottles of wine, a shepherd's pie and a basket filled with ripe-red strawberries.

"I bring them, my lord, from the King your Royal Cousin," he answered to the King's questions.

"Well done, indeed, my good Cunningson," said Witless. "Do remind me tomorrow to bestow upon you the Great Diamond-studded Cross of Unbridled Loyalty to the Crown, for you do deserve it."

"There are no more honours or decorations left in the coffers," said the High Chancellor uncertainly.

"No?… Ah, hmm… Well then, not to worry, I shall give you its title instead."

Cunningson stared once more at the precious stones of the crown, pursed his lips, and was about to reply.

The Prince, however, spoke first, and said to his father:

"My king and father, this man is lying. He most certainly did not go to the King our Royal Cousin. For when did he have the time to do so? It takes two days to go and as many to come back. Ask him where he did find all this food, and, until you know, may no one eat a single morsel!" he added, catching hold of Jealousia's hand just as she was about to dig her finger in the pie.

The King stood hesitant.

"Really? Does it really take two days to go to the realm of the King my Royal Cousin?" he asked of Cunningson.

He in turn became muddled and confused, started to blurt out some sort of explanation, froze with embarrassment and stopped.

"Father," said the Prince, "this food has been stolen. And I ask you as a favour that you oblige this man to return every item to the rightful owner."

The King pushed his crown nervously all the way to the back of his head, and rubbed his forehead with the heel of his hand. The very notion of losing his food did not appeal to him in the least.

"And how do you know, if I may ask, how long it takes for someone to go to the realm of the King our Royal Cousin?" he enquired sullenly.

"You sent me there once yourself, to ask for golden florins. Have you forgotten it, father? For I remember it well!" answered the Prince. "It took me two days to go, and two more to return. And four whole days did I have to wait there, till I could see the lord and master of the land. For the King our Royal Cousin does not grant audiences to beggars, except when the fancy takes him."

The proud aspect of his son began to irritate the King.

"Well, you went on foot. Cunningson surely took a horse," he snapped.

"There is no road, and a horse cannot pass by the rugged ridgeways. And even if there had been a road, still he would not have made it there and back again in such a short time."

"Dash it all! You are beginning seriously to annoy me!" yelled the King. "Let us then just say that he flew there! Stop bothering me, or I shall have you thrown in prison, future king or not."

And without further ado he sat down to supper, together with the women, Cunningson and the fool, who turned a cartwheel to show his joy, causing the little jingle bells of his motley-coloured garb to chime as he did so.

The Prince seized Little Irene's hand.

"Come with me," he said, "or I will suffocate in here!"

They went out together; in silence, with difficulty, tripping and stumbling in the darkness, they descended the mountain.

When they reached the valley, Little Irene stopped him.

"Where are we going?" she asked.

"Anywhere, as long as it is far away from this kingdom where such things can happen!"

"You mean to forsake your country?"

"Yes! Yes! Yes… I mean to leave this accursed land, and forget all about it!"

Little Irene made no reply. Her heart bled at the thought of leaving her fatherland, where she had been born and had grown up. Its squalor, its desolation, even its bad fortune, all these she loved, because this was her homeland.

Unspeaking, she followed her brother. And so they went on, for hours, and for more hours still, amidst the sharp stones and the crooked twigs of the undergrowth. Yet she was unaccustomed to such rough paths. Her feet, barely protected by her tattered silken slippers, were bruised all over. Her old sequined skirt, embroidered with golden thread, trailed on the ground, torn to shreds by the spiny thorns where it had been caught along the way.

She turned around and looked at her brother.

Lips pressed resolutely together, head held high, the Prince walked on, in full defiance of all pain and all tiredness. And the night breeze stroked his forehead, frolicking between the strands of his brown hair, which fell in rich, long locks all the way down to his gold-embroidered neckerchief.

He seemed to her so noble and beautiful that she embraced him.

"Yes! I shall come with you, wherever you may go!" she said to him. And with courage anew she set off again by his side. In a little while, however, her exhaustion vanquished her. She sat down at the edge of the road, and rested her head on her huddled knees.

"I cannot walk any farther!" she said faintly.

"Rest awhile," replied the Prince, "and then we will go on again."

At that, he climbed on a high rock to look around him. In the distance, through a thicket of trees, it seemed to him that he could see a light.

He scrambled down hurriedly from the rock, and ran to his sister.

"Get up, Little Irene, I have seen a light!" he cried out to her. "Come! It must be a house, and perhaps they will open their door to us, and give us shelter."

So they went on their way once more, towards the place where the light could be seen, till they arrived in front of a small, freshly whitewashed dwelling.

The Prince knocked at the door.

"Who is that?" asked a woman's voice inside.

"Please open your door to us," pleaded the Prince. "My sister and I ask for your hospitality, to warm ourselves up, and rest awhile."

The door opened, and an old woman with pure white hair and a face that had the sweetness of honey beckoned to them to enter.

"Welcome to the poor home of Mistress Wise," she said. "Come and sit down, my children, have a rest."

A young girl was lying asleep on a couch nearby. The old woman nudged her gently.

"Wake up, my good girl; guests have come to us. Get up and warm some milk, and bring along some rusks of bread."

The girl got up and lit the fire, warmed the milk. Then she poured it into two small mugs and smilingly placed these on the table in front of the famished siblings, together with a plate of rusks.

Little Irene, however, did not have time to eat, for she had fallen asleep on her chair. The two women lifted her in their arms and laid her on the couch.

"Get some sleep yourself, now, my young lord," said the old woman, "and tomorrow you can resume your journey. You have far to go?"

"Yes," replied the Prince, "I am going very far."

"A pity!" said the old woman pensively.

And with a sigh, she patted the young boy's curly head.

"A pity? Why so?" asked the Prince, taken aback.

The old woman, however, merely smiled.

"Good night to you, my child; sleep peacefully, it is late," she said.

And with her daughter they went into a small adjacent room and closed the door.

The Prince lay himself down to sleep on the hearthrug in front of the fireplace, and he did try his best to fall asleep. Yet for all his weariness, sleep would not come to him. The words of the old woman kept ringing in his head, now loudly and very distressingly, then again half-faded, as though coming to him from very far away.

"A pity!… A pity!… A pity…"

Why a pity? What did the old woman mean?

And with this thought he finally fell asleep.

The room was flooded with sunlight when he woke up in the morning. He got up and ran to the couch, where Little Irene was still lying, lost in reverie, although thoroughly awake.

"I was waiting for you," she said. "Come, let us go outside. It is so very beautiful outside!"

In her little kitchen garden, Mistress Wise was hanging the washed clothes out to dry, while her daughter, sitting on a little stool, was milking the cow.

They both smiled when they saw the two siblings.

"Knowledge, my good girl, give the children to drink some of the milk you have just milked, before it gets cold," said the old woman. "Do sit you down, my young lord and lady. You will have fine weather for your journey."

The Prince remembered the words she had said to him the previous night.

"Old mother," he said, "why do you think it a pity that I should go away?"

But the old woman had work to do in the house.

"I have no time just now, my young lord," she said. "Knowledge will answer your question. For she knows all such matters even better than I do myself."

And she went into her back kitchen to prepare the meal.

"Well then, you tell me, Knowledge," said again the Prince, "why does your mother say that it is a pity that I should be going away?"

The young girl hesitated awhile. Then she said cautiously:

"Because the King's son ought not to leave his land."

The Prince was startled.

"How can you tell who I am?" he asked.

"My mother can tell, she knows you. Once upon a while we too lived in the palace. But many years have gone by since then."

"And why did you go away?"

"Because other maids-in-waiting took my mother's place, and we could no longer stay. We left the palace, and stayed in a little house in the capital, at the foot of the mountain. But the new maids-in-waiting drove us away from there too, and so we left and went farther away, and farther still, and in the end we came here, to the edge of the kingdom, where no man sees us, no man concerns himself with us. And we live all by ourselves, in the solitude of the countryside, which used to be dense with green things and teeming with houses, and yet is now only barren stones and desolation."

"We too, we should come here!" said Little Irene. "It is so very peaceful and beautiful!"

"This is not a choice that is given to you," said Knowledge.

"Why not?" asked the Prince.

"Because you have to stay among your people."

"Oh, but I cannot!" said the Prince. "You cannot know what my people are like, the palace, this entire place…"

"Then set your people right again," replied the girl.

"I? How? I am only a child, I know nothing, I have learnt nothing, I *am* nothing."

The maiden considered him pensively.

"Why did you wish to leave?" she asked.

"Because I was in too much pain amidst the corruption and the dissolution of the palace."

"Well, then, that shows that you have something inside you worth more than all the things you have not learnt."

"What *do* I have?"

"You have an honourable soul, and dignity."

The Prince considered this for a while. Then he asked:

"And what good are these things to me?"

"They are good to you because you can use them to find in you the strength and the will to rebuild your nation."

"But how? How?!"

"How would I know to tell you?… Yet, if I were you, I would go back, and travel everywhere in the realm. Do

33

not remain locked up in the palace, go and talk with your people instead, come to know them, live by their side; listen to what the birds and the trees and the flowers have to say, the insects. If you only knew how many truths one may learn this way, how many examples one may find to show one the way!…"

The Prince paused thoughtfully for a very long time. Then he said:

"I *shall* go back, Knowledge, and I shall travel everywhere in the realm. Thank you."

He meant to say goodbye, but the maiden stopped him.

"Won't you stay awhile yet?" she asked. "You are all in tatters, you and your sister both. I have something I would like to give to the Princess as a gift, a thing that will serve her well."

She took out of her pocket a needle case and a bobbin of thread, and gave them to her.

"You see," she said, "it is no great gift, nor a costly one. Yet in its way it is priceless."

Little Irene stared at the thread and at the needles without understanding.

"What are these?" she asked, puzzled.

"What's that? You do not sew?" asked Knowledge.

"No, nor have I ever seen anyone else sew."

"Would you like to learn? Come, and I shall teach you."

And Knowledge sat on the front step of her house, took Little Irene's torn scarf, and darned all the holes.

Little Irene stared in amazement and bewilderment.

"Please let me have me the needle and thread! Oh, let me try too!" she begged.

She took the needle and darned her dress, then her silken slippers and the golden ribbons which tied up her brother's sandals, and which were all in knots, then his frayed neckerchief and his torn clothes.

She mended them so beautifully that when she had finished they all seemed to her as new.

"What fun this is!" she said excitedly. "And you, Knowledge, do you sew a great deal yourself?"

"I sew when I have finished all of my tasks."

"So you do more things in the house? Tell me, what?"

"All the housework: I tidy up, I wash, cook, knead bread and tend to the garden—"

"Fancy that!" interjected Little Irene. "I do nothing at all, all day long, and I am so very frightfully bored! This morning, for instance, until my brother was awake, I passed my hand again and again through the rays of the sun and watched the specks of dust leaping here and there, just so I could pass the time. I have no idea how to kill the endless hours of the day!"

Knowledge laughed.

"Do you wish to kill them, or to use them?" she asked.

"Isn't it the same?"

"No! Time always passes. But if you consume yourself in idle things, you waste it; whereas if you do work that has a purpose, you make good use of time."

"I've never thought of this before," said the Prince pensively. "To me too the hours appear endless!"

"And yet time is precious," replied Knowledge. "With what things do you busy yourself all day?"

"With no things! What can I busy myself with? Everyone lives for himself and is busy with himself alone; and I have need of nothing."

"And yet your country has need of you."

"Pah! Everyone looks after themselves, and manages in some way or other, lives any old how."

"You have put it well that everyone manages in some way or other, lives any old how," replied Knowledge, with sadness. Your country too manages in some way or other, any old how. And yet, will you allow yourself to be content with such a state of things?"

"What can I do?"

"If everyone thought less of his own individual self and worked more for the general good, they would see one day that they had still worked for themselves, and that instead of living any old how, they had managed in fact to live well."

"I do not understand," muttered the Prince.

Knowledge laughed.

"Have I clouded your heart?" she said. "Yet if you were to go back and live amongst your people, talk with them and listen to what they have to say, you would then understand infinitely better."

"I will go, as you say!" said the Prince earnestly.

The two siblings entered the back kitchen to bid farewell to Mistress Wise; they found her braising meat in a large pot.

"What? Will you not stay and taste my stew?" the old woman asked.

"Thank you kindly, but no," said the Prince. "I am in a hurry to go back."

The old woman cut them a thick slice of bread each, and thrust it affectionately into their pockets.

"The way is long," she said. "Godspeed to you, my children."

They bid goodbye to Knowledge, and then the siblings picked up once more the way back to the palace.

Every now and then Little Irene would turn her head to look at the small, hospitable white cottage, which was still visible through the leafy trees. And when that was lost from sight, she sighed heavily and looked at her brother who was walking straight ahead, with steady step, his head held high.

IV

On the Way Back

T HEY WALKED for many hours across the dry, boundless valley. Eventually they came to a desolate hamlet, where barely two or three dwellings still stood erect.

They stopped in front of the first and knocked at the door.

A middle-aged man with a crotchety face and unkempt clothes opened the door.

"What do you want?" he snapped.

"Just a place to sit down for a while. We are exhausted," replied the Prince.

"This is not an inn," said the man.

And he shut the door.

The siblings sat on the doorstep, and took out their bread to eat.

Before long, they heard the window open cautiously. They turned around, and saw the same man.

"What's the idea of sitting in front of my house like this?" he snapped again.

"Are we disturbing you?" asked the Prince, without rising.

"You most certainly are! Away with you!" retorted the man. "I don't like beggars."

"We ask you for nothing," said the Prince quietly.

The man became irascible.

"The doorstep is mine!" he yelled. "Be gone with you, or I shall give you a thrashing you'll never forget!"

The two siblings got up and went farther down the road. The spring sun, however, was strong and hot; seeking to find some shade, they returned to the back of the house, where amidst some rubble and ruins they lay down in a shady corner and fell asleep.

A light tapping noise awoke the Prince. It seemed to him that he could hear voices.

He rose carefully, peered through the stones without being seen, and saw the same inhospitable man: he was now speaking from his window to a child laden with a sack; his voice was hushed and secretive.

"Did anyone see you?" asked the man lowering his voice to a whisper.

"No, of course not! What am I, a fool to get caught?" answered the child. "But come, unload my burden, the sack is heavy!"

"What's in it?" asked the man, leaning out of the window to catch hold of it.

"A flask of wine, three apples, a shoe, two pies and a woolly hat."

"You found these things all together in one place?"

"No. Bittersuffering was at home when I went there. I snatched the wine and the apples, which he kept on the windowsill so they might stay fresh and cool, and took to my heels. The rest comes from Badluck. He was away to town where he was to be a witness at Miserlix's trial; so I took care of his house at my leisure." And with that the child broke into a guffaw. "Yet you have not seen the real booty," he went on, taking out of his pocket a silver watch. "I got this one last night, out of Miserlix's pocket. Ain't it a beauty?"

"Is that so? And where did you come across Miserlix?"

"Hah! I was there when the palace courtier with the chain thrust him down the mountain in order to take his haversack from him. So then down I scrambled myself as well, and, finding him unconscious, I groped about in his pockets and took his watch and two silver five-crown coins. Do I get no praise from you?"

"Come in," said the man delightedly. "Give me the silver coins, and you shall receive the very best praise! You have earned it!"

The window was then pulled shut and the child disappeared to the back of the house.

The Prince woke up his sister. His face was dark and clouded.

"Come," he said. "We must leave this place."

Little Irene got up and followed him.

"Who is chasing us away this time?" she asked.

"Little Irene," said the Prince, his eyebrows furrowing. "Do you know why the man did not want us on his doorstep just now?"

"No!"

"Because he is a fence, a receiver of stolen goods, and he was afraid we might see the boy who was bringing him the things he had stolen. And do you know what the dinner was that Cunningson brought to the palace last night? He stole it himself from some poor soul by the name of Miserlix, whom he even thrust down the mountainside so he might not talk. This is what goes on in our kingdom!"

"Heaven help us!" muttered Little Irene with tears in her eyes.

They walked through a small town with misshapen and squalid roads, the houses half in ruin.

Above a doorway they noticed some black letters. But neither knew how to read.

"Let us knock here and ask what this place is," said the Prince.

They knocked, and a pale, scrawny man opened the door to them, holding a book in his hand.

"What do you want, my children?" he said kindly.

"We wish to learn what this house is," said the Prince apologetically.

"This house? But it is written all up there, my children!" the man said, baffled, pointing to the letters above his door.

"We do not know how to read," said Little Irene with embarrassment.

"Aaah?…" said the man. "And yet it is the same sorry state everywhere in the realm; no one knows how to read any more."

And he explained to them that outside it was written "School of the State".

"A school!" exclaimed the Prince joyfully. "I have never seen a school, and I have always wanted to know what one is like! But… where are the pupils?"

The man scratched his ear, hesitated, and finally said:

"They are… they are away at present."

"And at what time will they be back for their lessons? I should like to see them," said the Prince.

"But… But they do not have lessons…" answered the man hesitantly.

And seeing the puzzlement in the boy's eyes:

"Well, so be it… Yes, that's right, I do not give them lessons!" he burst out bitterly. "As if it were easy to do the proper thing in this place! The State appointed me as teacher, and entrusted the children to me so I might teach them their letters. Only the State forgets to pay me, forgets that I too have needs, that I must eat and clothe myself! The children come but I do not give them lessons. I take them to my kitchen garden to work the soil, so I might have my bread, and I send them to the woods to pick strawberries, or arbutus berries, or other seasonal fruit. I am a man too, you know! I too must live!"

All this the schoolmaster said with great grief, his eyes brimming with tears.

The Prince gazed at him, lost in thought. His face was grave.

"And who forces you to stay on as schoolmaster?" he asked finally.

"What else could I do? I would die out in the cold. Here at least I have a house!"

"So then you do accept the house," said the Prince, his eyes flaring, "even though you do not fulfil your duty!"

The schoolmaster smiled.

"As if that were easy now!" he said quietly. "You are but a child! You do not know what life is like, and you think it is simple and easy to do your duty, to work unrewarded for the benefit of others! Only, in order to do your duty, my boy, you need sometimes to make a heroic sacrifice of yourself. And not everyone is a hero in this world."

The Prince went out, without giving an answer.

Many thoughts, and ever more thoughts, stumbled and tripped in his mind. It seemed to him that his eyes were looking at new worlds.

There was a long moment of silence, while he held his sister's hand.

"Self-sacrifice!" he murmured. "You heard that, Little Irene? It takes, he said, a heroic act of self-sacrifice, and not everyone is a hero... Do you recall the words of Knowledge, that by labouring for the common good, we benefit ourselves in the end? I am afraid that in our country no one ever learnt that. Each of us seeks to profit for himself alone, or, at the very least, to be left in peace..."

"Why do you say this, brother?"

"Because we too are no different. Neither you nor I nor anyone else from the palace ever did anything for the common good… Yes, Little Irene, this is how the State was brought to its ruin…"

Brother and sister continued their way without speaking, each lost in thought.

They reached another hamlet, as impoverished and deserted as the first.

In a small garden, unkempt, overgrown, untilled, there sat, next to some half-parched furrow weeds, a poorly dressed little old man; he was busy wool-gathering and playing with a rosary to pass the time.

"A very good day to you," he said as brother and sister went past.

"Good afternoon to you, grandfather," replied the Prince. "Would you let us sit a little in your garden, to rest?"

"You most certainly may, my children. Why don't you come in indeed, share a word or two with old Penniless here, so I may forget my troubles?" answered the old man.

They entered the garden, and sat on the bench next to him.

"It distresses me deeply that I have nothing left to offer you," said the old man. "Only they stole from me the one thing that I had, wretch that I am, some few fresh raspberries, which were my pride and joy! Where are you headed, my young lord and lady?"

"To the capital," replied Little Irene.

"Is that so? You travel far. And what will you do in the capital?"

"We go to find work," said the Prince.

The old man barely suppressed a smile:

"You will only be wasting your time, my children. There is no work to be found in the capital any more."

"Why?"

"Because no one is so foolish as to work so that he may earn the bread that his neighbour will eat in his stead."

And he pointed all around him to the thorny thistles and the weeds that covered the earth.

"The entire country prospers in this same way, like my little garden here," he went on. Once upon a while, this tiny corner of the earth was blessed by God. Yet who would know it now? My boy is gone away, I am left alone, and I am tired of working for the benefit of others."

"Why did your son go away?" asked the Prince.

"What else might he do here? Together we cultivated our fields, which stretched as far as there yonder, and we sold our yield to the neighbouring villages. We even grew oranges, apples and grapes. The choicest greens and fruit ripened here, before they did so anywhere else. The palace would send here for its provisions of all the fine things it wanted. But things changed, our good King died, and his son is having forty winks. That is why we are all going to the devil."

"Why do you say he is having forty winks?" asked Little Irene, flushing red, her eyes filling with tears.

"Well, he may not be really asleep and dead to the world, but it amounts to much the same thing, since he only knew how to command evening balls, and great feasts; and he never cared about work of any sort, till he consumed all he had, and more that he did not—"

"This does not tell us why your son went away," interrupted the Prince, who did not wish to hear more about his father.

"How does it not? Back then, in the good times, when Prudentius I was still alive, the palace paid for what it received. And it paid well. Afterwards, it no longer paid, but it still received. So, hurriedly and furtively, we would harvest and send away the choicest things in the land, so we might earn some money at least. Yet the roads, with no one to care for them, fell to ruin, our carts would smash in the ditches. Before long, not even our beasts of burden could get through. Our grain would rot in the storehouses, or the palace would feed on it, without paying. Poverty and misery fell upon the land, commerce was ruined, the storehouses crumbled and collapsed, the young men left, the best went to foreign lands, others went to the capital, to become, they said, scientists, and are still there now, starving. The worst stayed behind and are scraping a living by making themselves a burden to their fellow men. He got fed up, my son, he sold our fields for a pittance, left me the money and he too then went abroad. I used to cultivate my garden, growing my own vegetables, buying my own bread. But no one is safe any longer!"

"What do they do to you?" asked Little Irene.

"What don't they do to us, you might well ask, my girl! The village has been deserted, there is no man left to protect us, they steal whatever is in our gardens, and out of spite they destroy our trees and our vegetables. Just to show you, only last night they stole the few raspberries that were ripening slowly on my bramble hedge. And that's not all! They also hacked the entire plant to pieces and pulled it out of its roots! I am fed up, I have given up, and I too live on just any old how, till my days are spent and I may find peace from the troubles of this world. Such is my lot."

"And the money that your son left you?" asked Little Irene.

"Stolen, my girl, gone, never to be seen again! You think there will be money left, when they do not even leave us our bread?"

"How come you do not go to court?" asked the Prince outraged. "Why then do we have judges?"

Penniless laughed.

"The judges are not for our sort," he said. "They are for the rich, who fill their pockets. From us, the have-nots, they can make no profit. Go, if you want, to the trial of Miserlix, as you are headed to the capital and are curious to know. There you shall hear justice being pronounced."

"I shall go indeed," said the Prince. "I wish to see with my own eyes what you have said."

"Do go, my boy, and witness with your eyes, hear with your own ears. The trials take place in the square, under the great plane tree."

The two siblings bid farewell to the old man, and took the road to the capital.

They arrived late. The sun had descended behind the mountain, the trial, at this hour, was over.

The Judge, wrapped in his frayed red coat, which had lost its original colour with the passing of time, was getting up to go home, while two scruffy policemen were trailing behind them a shabbily dressed, pale man, hands in shackles, leading him away to prison. His head was bandaged with a scarf, and, full of grief, he held tightly in his arms his daughter, who was crying with heavy sobs.

"Who is this man?" asked the Prince.

"It is Miserlix, the blacksmith," answered one of the bystanders.

"Why are they taking him to prison?"

"Bless me if I know! He stole, so they say, some hens. I did not understand very well, they did not say much, but they have sentenced him to two years in prison. Yet he was a fool, if ever there was one! He claimed that some palace courtier stole chickens, wine and I know not what else from him, then sent him rolling down the mountain slope where he split his head. Someone also stole from him, he says, his watch and two silver five-crown coins. You may be sure that His Excellency, Judge Faintheart, ticked him off all right, called him a liar and a thief. He then told us that not only

48

was it not true that his chickens had been stolen, but that it was Miserlix himself who had stolen them, I know not where from. The Judge gave orders for him to be beaten till he confessed the truth. Miserlix then took fright, and asked them not to beat him; he would agree to go to prison, and they could say what they liked, even that it was he who had stolen the hens. Couldn't he have stayed quietly in his corner, the fool, instead of seeking courts and justice?!"

"But this is shameful! It is downright sinful!" the Prince cried, furious.

"Shameful or not, sinful or not, that's the court of justice for you," answered the other.

"No, this is not what the court of justice should be!" said the Prince. "Where does the Judge live?"

They pointed out the house to him, and he ran and knocked at the door, pulling Little Irene by the hand.

The Judge was already back by then, and was sitting at his table eating mackerels with relish, and drinking brandy made from mastic.

"Who goes there?" he shouted with his mouth full, not bothering to get up.

"Open up!" ordered the Prince. "I have things to say to you concerning Miserlix."

"Oh, go away, leave me alone!" replied the Judge, biting into another crunchy mackerel.

"*Open up!*" shouted the Prince. "Or I swear to you, before the sun has risen, I will have your head for this."

"Heavens!" exclaimed Faintheart. "It has to be the King!"

Trembling like a leaf, he rushed to open the door. Yet when he saw the two children before him, his fright turned to rage.

"What's the meaning of this? Are you trying to make a fool of me?" he asked snappishly. "Get out of here right now, or I shall have you both thrown into prison."

Calmly, yet resolutely, the Prince pushed him aside, and entered the house with his sister.

"I give you fair warning, Master Faintheart, to listen to me and to listen well. Close the door and come here."

The boy's imperious tone made Faintheart cower and shrink.

"What do you want?" he asked, subdued.

"I want you to get Miserlix out of prison, at once!"

"All right, all right, there is enough time for that," said the Judge lightly. "Those mackerels are still nicely warm and scrumptious. Wouldn't you like one?"

"I am not in a mood for jokes, Master Faintheart," said the Prince sternly. "Either you get Miserlix out of prison at once, or you will be dealing with me."

"Aaaah! Enough is enough; you are starting to get on my nerves!" said the Judge, who was beginning to get cross once more. "Would you in fact mind telling me who Your Greatness might be, that you should dare make such threats?"

"I am the King's son and I command you!" replied the Prince, furious in his turn.

Master Faintheart lost his wits at that. He made as though to bow; and was left fixed on the spot in that position, folded in two.

"Order… Order thine servant…" he muttered, quivering.

"You are to set Miserlix free at once!" commanded the Prince.

"At once, my lord!"

"And send out men to arrest the High Chancellor and throw him into prison in his place, for you know well that it was he who stole the chickens, and not Miserlix."

Master Faintheart fell on his knees.

"My lord, spare me! Do not ask of me such things. Who told you the truth I do not know, but if you know this much, you certainly know more! Cunningson is a powerful man! How could I possibly arrest him?"

"He is a thief!"

"Yet he has many florins!"

"How did he come by them? He has nothing!"

"He has the control of the palace coffers. He does as he likes!"

"He has nothing, I tell you. He was obliged to sell his golden chain of state in order to provide food for the palace for two days—for all that the chain is not even his to sell, but only the insignia of his rank. Yet, even if he did have many florins, this should not hinder you from arresting him."

Master Faintheart began to whimper.

"I cannot, he will destroy me, he is the High Chancellor, and has the King's full trust. Heed my words, and spare me, for in truth I know not myself what course to take! When Miserlix came to me and voiced his grievances, and described to me the palace courtier who had thrown him downhill and robbed him of his haversack, at once I realized who it was, for he wore, as he said, a chain. The whole affair caused me great distress, because I did not wish to find myself up against the High Chancellor, and my desire was to convince Miserlix to keep this quiet. Yet in vain! That one wanted justice to be done, and would not be quietened down!"

"Good for him!" said the Prince. "It would have been most cowardly had he kept silent!"

"So then," continued Master Faintheart, "I sent word immediately to Cunningson in secret, to tell him to return the stolen sack, so that Miserlix might then keep quiet. Only, he rushed here at once, and told me that unless I found a way to throw Miserlix into prison, he would charge me with stealing the chain myself, and then I would have my head cut off."

"You *are* a coward! Why would you alert him in secret?"

"I was afraid of him!"

"You should not have been afraid! No one would have believed that you had stolen the chain, since he himself has sold it to provide food for the palace."

"He did not sell it on behalf of the palace," said the Judge in a very small voice. "And they would have certainly believed that I had stolen it myself."

"How is that so?"

"Because… because he had given the chain to me, to sell on his behalf… I made out a document in his name… and because… the chain… I still had it in my house."

"From this sale, then, you yourself received no profit?" asked the Prince, stressing each syllable one by one.

The Judge did not reply, only bowed his head even lower.

With arms crossed, the Prince stood gazing at the man as he knelt before him, most utterly contemptible, humiliated.

"You are right to be afraid," he said at last, filling his voice with all the disgust that swelled up in his heart. "One blackguard cannot pass judgement on another blackguard. You two are birds of a feather!"

And, seizing a horsewhip that hung on the wall:

"March ahead," he commanded angrily. "Take your keys and open the door of the prison at once, or else your shoulders shall know whether this sting has the power to hurt or not!"

Trembling from head to toe, out came the Judge; he went to the jailor's house, took the keys, and from there proceeded to the prison.

The Prince and Little Irene had gone with him.

Outside the door, down on the dusty earth, a girl wailed inconsolably.

The Prince recognized her.

"Do not cry," he said compassionately. "Your father will return home to you this evening. Go in and take him."

Master Faintheart opened the door and the girl threw herself at her father's neck, pulling him outside.

"To whom do I owe my freedom?" asked Miserlix with a tremulous voice, once he had recovered from the first surge of emotions.

"To this boy," answered the girl, pointing at the Prince.

Miserlix bowed and kissed the threadbare, gold-embroidered robes.

"May the heavens repay you for it!" he said, and his heart was in his words. "If ever you may need a true friend, remember me."

And, supporting himself upon his daughter's arm, he walked towards his house.

"Now go and eat your mackerel," said the Prince contemptuously to the Judge, "and never again show yourself before me, for I will have you know that you won't escape the horse's whip a second time."

Master Faintheart did not wait to be told twice, and took to his heels.

It was now completely dark. Brother and sister, hungry, tired, dragged their feet onwards.

"Where do we go now?" asked Little Irene.

"To the palace," her brother replied. "I must settle Master Cunningson's affairs."

And they took the way uphill, climbing the mountain.

V

The Gift of the King the Royal Uncle

N O SOONER had they approached the palace than they heard angry voices and snivelling whimpers.

"It was *her*, *she* is the one who tore my scarf!" Jealousia was screaming.

"And I shall also *scratch* and *tear* at your face!" came the riposte of Spitefulnia.

"Same as ever!" said the Prince sorrowfully.

And the two siblings hurried onwards to enter the palace, where the screams could be heard louder and louder.

Inside the room the sight was heart-rending. The two sisters, bereft of scarves and enraged, held one another by the hair and were hitting each other with mad fury. With his head thrown back so he could see from underneath his crown, which had slipped all the way down to the tip of his nose, the King was striving to separate them, while one of the maids-in-waiting, the fair, chubby one, lay asleep on the threadbare cushions of the sofa, utterly undisturbed by all the racket and commotion; and the other, scrawny and dark, profiting from the general upheaval, was gobbling down an apple pie which had been served for the King.

Seated on the floor, the Queen busied herself with the embellishment of her skirt, using shards of glass from a broken bottle and taking no notice of the general mayhem around her. By her side stood the High Chancellor with two equerries, each of whom was holding a covered basket, waiting for the squabble to cease, so they might hold audience with the King.

Little Irene threw herself between her sisters.

"Stop, in God's name, *stop*!" she pleaded. "Your antics are most shameful! Your screams can be heard far beyond the palace walls!"

The princesses stopped, startled, and each let go of the other's hair.

"Where did you come from, little one?" they asked, both at once.

The King lifted the crown from his nose, and smiled at Little Irene.

"Welcome, you!" he said, pacified. "Have you been out for a stroll? We have not seen you at all today."

The Queen, busy with her shards of glass, did not even turn to look.

"She was with me," said the Prince. "And I wish to have a word with you at once, father."

"Is that so? You are here too? And where might you have been wandering?" asked the King.

"In many places," replied the Prince. "And I have learnt a few things that you need to know."

"If they be pleasant and amusing, do tell them at once, otherwise leave them for later. Dark concerns bore me immensely."

And he sat in his armchair, wiping his forehead with the sleeve of his shirt, which hung out loose through a slit in his robes.

"No, father," answered the Prince. "They are neither pleasant nor amusing. Yet you *must* hear them."

The King shooed him away with a gesture of his hand.

"Later, you'll tell me everything then. Come here yourself, now, Cunningson, and tell me what might be the business of these two basket-bearing men."

The High Chancellor drew nearer and bowed.

"These are the two equerries whom I had sent last week to the neighbouring kingdoms," he explained. "They have returned at last, and bring the answers of the rulers, your royal relatives."

"Bid them approach," ordered the King.

"Polydorus!" called out the High Chancellor.

The first equerry set down his basket and knelt before his sovereign.

"My lord," he said, "I went to His Majesty your Royal Cousin and told him all that His Excellency the High Chancellor had commanded me to say. I had barely spoken the first words, and he threw insults at me, threatened to have me hanged and thrown to his dogs to be devoured by them. He then had me sent for again, and asked me many questions about the palace and about Your Majesty. In the end he told me to take this basket and to bring it to you, this being, however, the last gift he will send to you, for he is, he said, building ships and buying swords, and has no florins to spare to send abroad."

The King blazed up, was dismayed and then became furious.

"The impudence of him!" he thundered, menacing his invisible relative with his clenched fist. "He is building ships and buying swords, or so he claims! Let him just dare say so once more, and I shall pour into his kingdom an army of a hundred thousand, and I shall send down the river my colossal fleet, so that he will be stunned with terror…"

Then, suddenly changing tone:

"Uncover the basket, Cunningson," he continued, "and see if there is anything good to eat inside. This talk about business has given me an appetite, and my throat is parched."

Cunningson unpicked the string with which the cover had been sewn onto the basket, opened it, and proffered it to the King; he, with great haste, pushed aside some stalks of hay and revealed a tiny basket containing a few eggs.

"What are these?!" he bellowed peevishly.

"These are eggs, my lord," said the High Chancellor very respectfully.

"I can see that, you idiot! I am not asking you to tell me what they are called!… Empty out the hay, and look underneath. There must be more things, a hidden treasure perhaps…"

The High Chancellor took out the basket of eggs, set it down beside him and carefully fumbled through the hay.

But he found nothing.

"You are nothing but a nincompoop!" said the King uneasily. "I am certain that I shall find the treasure myself."

And kneeling beside the basket, he plunged half inside it.

In the meantime, and seeing that everyone's attention was turned upon the gift of the King the Royal Cousin, the dark-haired maid-in-waiting drew stealthily nearer, and, grabbing some eggs, shoved them in her pocket.

The Prince, standing cross-armed nearby, saw this, but he did not speak. He gazed at the scene with deeply felt disgust.

Nothing else could be found in the basket, and the King sat back in his armchair, sulky and snappish.

"You there, come here as well," he said to the second equerry. "Tell me how you fared at the palace of the King my Royal Uncle."

The equerry Polycarpus approached with his basket, and, as Polydorus had done before him, knelt in front of the King.

"My lord, when the King your Royal Uncle heard all that His Excellency the High Chancellor had bid me say, he smiled, and asked me to wait outside while he took counsel with his jester, who is, he says, his best advisor; he wanted to decide what he might send you, which would be of the greatest benefit to you. He then sent for me and gave me this sealed hamper and a letter that I have brought to you."

"Hand it over," said the King, greatly pleased. "He at least has royal manners!"

He took the letter, opened it, perched his spectacles securely on the bridge of his nose, and began to read it out:

Most Illustrious King and Nephew,

I have been informed of your news with great joy, and also that things are not going so very well in that kingdom of yours. And thus I now finally have the opportunity of being of good use to you, and of sending you a gift. My reasoning is that if I send you golden florins, you shall spend them, and they will run out. If, on the other hand, I send you things to eat, whether cooked or uncooked, they shall be eaten, and again all too swiftly consumed. If I send you clothes, with time they will become threadbare. So, then, I have sent you a gift which you shall keep for ever, a gift proportionate to your worth, most illustrious King and Nephew, such a gift, that upon looking at it you shall feel instantly how great my esteem is for you, and you will also realize how significant your existence is to the rest of the world.

As ever,

The King your Royal Uncle

"There! *This* is a man!" cried the King excitedly. "See a letter written with courteousness and good sense! Proportionate, he writes, to my worth, do all of you hear this well? What do you stand there for, Cunningson, you nincompoop? Why don't you open up the basket?"

Cunningson cut the strings and uncovered a parcel wrapped in a red silk scarf, intricately worked with gold and silver patterns.

The red colour caught the eye of the Queen, who had remained indifferent until then to all the goings-on.

She got up hurriedly, abandoning her glass shards, and ran to the King.

"Oh, how lovely, how dazzlingly flamboyant!" she said. "You keep the gift, my king, but do give me the scarf so I may make a pretty bonnet."

"Have it you shall, my lady," said the King with joy. "I will give you anything you desire now! Cunningson, place the parcel on the table. Indeed, I wish to open it myself."

He secured his crown onto his head, wrapped himself with great dignity in his discoloured mantle, and drew near the table.

With enormous care, he undid the knots of the scarf. A parchment covered the gift, and the King read out pompously and thunderously the words written upon it with gold ink:

If you understand my meaning, it shall be to your benefit.

"Careful!" cautioned the King. "You see that there is a secret meaning concealed in here. To me has been bestowed the glory of discovering it. Move aside!"

And with a gesture of great majesty he lifted the parchment—unveiling a donkey's head with a tin crown between its pointed ears!

A general guffaw broke out around the table. The King alone remained speechless, his mouth agape, his eyes bulging, while the Queen, seizing the scarf, was hastening to her mirror to wrap it over her head.

The Prince too had drawn closer, his face grown ashen, looking now at his father, and now at the donkey's head. Then suddenly, hiding his face in his hands, he leant against the windowsill and burst into tears.

The King heard his son's sobs in the midst of everyone else's laughter. He turned around, his face transformed.

"Who weeps?" he asked.

His eyes fell upon the young man, standing against the window, and with shaky steps he advanced towards him, placing his hand heavily upon his child's shoulder.

"You," he said, "*you* are *truly* noble! You felt the insult hurled against your father. Blessed may you be!"

And for the first time in his life, the old King pulled his son into his arms and gave him a hearty kiss.

Once the first surge of emotions had died down, and he had dried his eyes and blown his nose, the King returned to the table and called his son to him.

"Come, my boy," he said. "In the future, you shall rule with me. It is you who will help me pay back the insult."

His gaze fell upon the donkey's head.

"Take it outside! Remove it from here!" he cried, covering his eyes.

The High Chancellor charged forward to take it. But the Prince stretched out his arm and stopped him.

"No!" he said. "My father and my king, change your command, and allow me, on the contrary, to put it where all of us may see it every day, every hour, until we have redeemed ourselves of our shame."

"My child, what are you saying?!" groaned the King.

"The donkey's head irks you, father, because we are not worthy right now to return the gift to its sender. Yet if we destroy it, we shall forget it. And we must not forget it. Let it remain here."

And he took the donkey's head, and hung it from a tarnished gilded hook above a gold-leaf cabinet with one missing leg, the most ostentatious piece of furniture in the entire room.

"And now, Master Cunningson," said the Prince, turning to the High Chancellor, "we have some business to settle between us."

The High Chancellor turned pale.

"My lord," he said uneasily, bowing to the ground before the King. "Do you not think that affairs of state are better dealt with by us alone, without the assistance of His Highness the Prince? He is still so very young, your royal son, he has learnt nothing yet."

The King hesitated and glanced at his boy.

"My King and father," said the Prince. "If this request has your approval, I shall leave. But before I go, ask this man what he did with the golden chain that you entrusted to him, as a mark of his rank and office."

"He sold it," replied the King, "to provide us with things to eat."

"He did not sell it, father, and if you were to go to the house of Faintheart the Judge, who is his accomplice, you would find it there…"

He had no time to finish his sentence.

With a great leap, the High Chancellor was out of the window, vanishing in the darkness of the night.

After him leapt the Prince, pursuing him in the dark, amidst the rocks and stones.

Stumbling and rolling, Cunningson flapped down the mountain towards the capital, but he was unaccustomed to running, and the Prince gained fast upon him.

He was reaching out to seize hold of him at last, when all of a sudden the High Chancellor lost his wits completely; in a mad attempt to escape he turned towards the crevasse, tripped and plummeted over the precipice, smashing his bones in the course of his fall against the protruding rocks.

When he returned to the palace once again, the Prince was greeted by the King and Little Irene; they stood with the two equerries by the entry gate of the donjon tower, calling out to him anxiously.

"Let us go to bed, my child," the King said to him. "It is late, and my head aches…"

"You go to bed, father, for I cannot," replied the Prince breathlessly. "Only give me your two equerries. Cunningson fell over the precipice, and I must go to Faintheart's house at once, on the off-chance that I might find the golden chain still there. It was very foolish of me not to take it then and there, when I was at his house, and had a hold on him! We now have great need of florins, many florins, and we have none."

"What do you need florins for, my son?" said the King indifferently. "Can't you see how tired we all are?…"

"Do not forget the gift of the King our Royal Uncle, father," said the Prince gravely.

At that, the King lowered his head, and raised no more objections.

The Prince took the two equerries and hurried to Master Faintheart's house in the capital.

None of the windows had any light.

They knocked at the door, yet no one answered from inside. They knocked a second time, and still there was no answer.

"Break down the door," ordered the Prince.

At that, the three men put all their strength together, and succeeded, after great effort, in breaking down the door.

The house was pitch dark. Only in the back kitchen was there a feeble glimmer of light, where some logs were burning away in a brazier, and a few mackerels were turning into charcoal amongst the cinders.

The Prince lit a torch and with his companions searched throughout the house. But he found no one.

On the table, next to a bottle of sweet mastic wine, he saw a folded sheet of paper. He unfolded it, yet he did not know how to read it; so he folded it back again and put it in his pocket.

He searched everywhere, yet all the drawers were empty; he found nothing. He then went out with the two equerries, and returned to the palace.

Everyone was asleep. Only Little Irene was still up, waiting for him.

"Why aren't you in bed, too?" her brother asked fondly.

Little Irene smiled.

"I have been waiting for you, my brother, and guess what I have been doing? I have mended father's mantle, and his tattered robes, patched up the torn skirt of Spitefulnia and the ripped scarf of Jealousia, which gave rise to today's quarrel."

The Prince kissed her.

"I see you have begun to put into good practice the advice of Knowledge," he said. "But tell me, have you had anything to eat?"

Little Irene took a chunk of bread out of her pocket and gave it to him bleakly.

"I could find nothing more! My dinner too was a piece like this one. I saved half for you."

"And the eggs—those famous, celebrated eggs—of the King our Royal Cousin? Did they not give you any?"

Little Irene shook her head.

"There were only a few eggs," she replied, "and our sisters have a fine appetite… And then father too was hungry…"

"I see," said the Prince. "Everyone ate, except for you."

The siblings embraced one another, and went to their respective rooms. They fell asleep instantly, and in the sweetness of their slumber forgot for a few hours life's adversities and its bitter twists and turns.

VI

Army and Navy Present and Correct!

A T DAYBREAK the Prince woke up Little Irene. "Come with me," he said. "I shall go and fetch the day's food before the others wake up."

"Where are we going?" asked his sister.

"To the woods. Take a small basket with you; we shall gather anything that we find along the way."

With a light step, the siblings descended the mountain; all of a sudden, a strange noise drew their attention.

Brother and sister paused to listen. "What is that sound?" asked Little Irene.

"It appears to be the clinking of a small goat bell," replied the Prince.

"A goat bell in these parts? How could that be so? There are no goats anywhere nearby!"

They advanced a little farther; and yet again they heard the jingle of a small bell.

Little Irene looked about her—she could see nothing, however, so she approached the ridge of the precipice.

Yet when she leant forward to see, she let out a scream and pulled herself back.

"What is the matter?" asked the Prince, peering out beside her.

Down below, at the foot of the mountain, lay the corpse of the High Chancellor, just as it had fallen in the chasm; and, in a circle around it, there pranced about like a monkey a little man, half-black, half-yellow, now pulling himself straight, then again squatting low beside the body.

His every movement was accompanied by the tinkling of jingle bells.

"It is a dead man!" whispered Little Irene fearfully.

"It is Cunningson," replied the Prince, "and that's the court jester. What is he doing there, though, I wonder? It is as though he were trying to lift him up and carry him away all by himself…"

All of a sudden, the dwarf crouched over the dead man, ripped his shirt open, thrust his hand inside, and with a squeal and a giggle he rose up again, and ran to the vale, and from thence to the capital, as fast as his crooked little bowed legs would take him.

"What did he do?" asked Little Irene, shaking all over. "What did he do to Cunningson?"

"I could not make out," replied the Prince, "but then again the jester has always been a little unhinged… Come, Little Irene, do not be so frightened!"

They picked up their trail once again, towards the vale, which they descended heading towards the woods.

It was heavenly at that time of the day. The small birds were singing their morning song, which rose up like a prayer to the gentle sky above. The flowers spread their sweet fragrance all around them, and a thousand translucent droplets had caught themselves on every leaf, every blade of grass, like diamonds of incalculable worth.

Nature was waking up everywhere to the first rays of the sun. A chaffinch flew low, seeking a blade of hay, or a downy feather, with which to build its nest. The bees fluttered about, humming lovingly around the dewy wild flowers, and the bramble bush was spreading forth its twigs and branches, heavy with fruit, as though offering them up to the famished siblings.

"Oh, what lovely blackberries!" exclaimed Little Irene. "Come, let us gather them all."

The Prince, however, remained crouched close to the ground, observing the comings and goings of the ants, which followed always the same path, whether they were coming or going, stopping here and there as though to chat to one another, then departing again in haste, without ever stepping out of their file. A few were laden with some grain or insect, and the Prince remarked that these ones were all travelling to the same place, whereas the ones returning from it never carried anything at all.

"Come here, Little Irene," he called, "come! Let us find out where the ants are taking their load!"

And stooping low, close upon the ground, brother and sister followed the living line, which terminated at a little hole, where all the ants of burden would make their way in, and would come out again afterwards without their load, going away once more to find some other thing to carry.

"How strange, indeed," said Little Irene. "Look, they do not eat their food; instead they hide it inside the hole."

"The hole is their nest," replied the Prince—and he went on, deeply absorbed in thought. "Do you recall the words of Knowledge, that by living close to nature one may learn many things? Here then is the first lesson that the ant teaches us. It will not simply collect its daily meal; instead, it makes a deposit of food in its nest, perhaps for the more difficult times ahead…"

"Yes, indeed," said Little Irene with admiration. "It would be a good thing if we did the same ourselves. Yet what may we gather? The blackberries will rot, they will not keep!"

"We must do things altogether differently," replied the Prince, "if we wish to be ready to face the storms and tempests, be prepared when evil times might fall upon us."

Brother and sister continued on their way, talking and gathering whatever fruit they found on the trees and low shrubs.

Before long, they came to a lake, half-concealed under the trees and beneath the thickets of reeds. A flock of frightened wild ducks flew up and left with a tremendous flapping of wings.

"Ducks!" cried out the Prince joyfully. "Since this is where they nest, we should find lots of eggs!"

Indeed, it did not take them long to find the nests, and to collect so many eggs that, once the basket was full, they had to tie their neckerchiefs into makeshift pouches and fill these too.

"What a shame that you do not have a bow!" said Little Irene. "You might have killed a wild duck or two. Look, not all of them are gone, there are still some over there amongst the reeds."

"I may not have a bow, but I have a sling," came the cheerful reply of the Prince.

And with one shot he killed a duck that was nervously poking its head out from among the reeds to take a look at the two siblings.

The hunt exhilarated him. He took off his sandals and leapt into the water to retrieve the dead bird. Then he took aim and killed more wild waterfowl.

When he had gathered a good few, he trussed them up together by threading a long bulrush through their beaks, and, slinging them over his shoulder, he headed full of good merriment towards the palace with his sister.

In the valley they also picked a bunch of wild greens.

"Now I have all I need for my stew," said Little Irene. "Today we shall have a royal feast!"

"At least our meal will have been honourably earned," came her brother's reply.

When they reached the palace, everyone was still asleep.

They went into the scullery to set down their load, and there they found the equerry Polycarpus, lying asleep before the hearth.

The scullery was filthy and cluttered. The pots had been left unwashed; some chipped plates were strewn haphazardly here and there, together with dirty glasses.

Little Irene rolled up her sleeves, and began to put things in order.

"What are you going to do?" asked the Prince.

"What Knowledge herself would have done in my position," replied Little Irene. "I shall first clean up all this mess, and then I will cook the birds, just as I saw Mistress Wise do with the meat."

The Prince gave her a hearty embrace.

"Here's to you, little sister," he said. "With you by my side, I feel I shall fulfil my purpose."

"What purpose is that?"

"To send that donkey's head back to its donor."

Their talk had awakened Polycarpus. He saw the siblings, and at that he got up hastily, bowed deeply, and was about to leave the room. But seeing Little Irene picking up the glasses, he stopped in his tracks, and his surprise turned into bewilderment when he then saw her wash them and dry them.

He flushed red and ran to take them away from her hands.

"This will not do, my young royal mistress! This is no work fit for your little hands!" he said, his voice cracking.

Little Irene laughed.

"And why ever not?" she asked.

"Because this is the work of the undercook!"

"And where might the undercook be?"

"He is asleep, or out revelling somewhere," he replied.

"You see, then? It is I who must do this, since there is no one else to do the task. The scullery has to be scrubbed clean, and the meal has to be cooked. Since the head cook and the undercook are absent, I shall take their place."

The equerry had now turned bright scarlet.

"Well… Well…" he began, and stopped.

"Well, what?" asked Little Irene.

"Well then, let me help you, my young royal mistress! If you yourself will stoop to such a task, then so shall I."

He seized a pail and broom, and with great zeal began to scrub the floor of the scullery, while Little Irene plucked the birds.

The Prince, however, hearing voices from the royal chambers, went to deliver to his father the letter that he had found on Faintheart's table.

The family were all gathered in the dining hall, and when the Prince entered they greeted him with one voice:

"Come closer, and hear about the miracle."

The King strolled once, then twice before him, and then, proudly displaying his mantle, asked:

"Can you see anything new?"

"No," answered the Prince.

"How so, no?" exclaimed Jealousia. "Can't you see that some mighty monarch has sent us new clothes? He sent a skirt to Spitefulnia, new robes and a mantle to the King, and a beautiful scarf to me, just like the one that that harridan sister of mine tore yesterday."

Thankfully, Spitefulnia was busy admiring her skirt, so that she did not hear Jealousia's words.

The Prince laughed.

"Truly, there has been a miracle," he said, "but you should seek its agent not outside, but inside this palace. Your clothes are the same, only a little fairy has darned them for you."

"A fairy!" said the Queen ecstatically, clasping her fine, beautiful hands together. "Oh, did you see her? And did she not bring me some emerald bracelet, such as that of the Queen my Royal Aunt?"

"That would have been a hard task to perform," replied the Prince. "Little Irene has nimble fingers, but no florins!"

Explanations were called for. And so the Prince told them the story of how Little Irene had waited up for him during the night, while everyone else was asleep, and how she had sat down and darned everyone else's clothes.

The Queen was outraged.

"My daughter, a seamstress!" she cried out. "But this is unheard of! Is this how low my daughter, the royal Princess, has fallen?"

With that, she suffered one of her attacks of nerves, and had to leave the room.

"How perfectly vulgar!" said the fair-haired maid-in-waiting, disgusted. "I can't *possibly* have anything to do with her any longer, after such conduct!"

And most majestically, she sprawled herself on the sofa.

"*Why* must you be so daft?" whispered the other to her. "On the contrary, cajole her and pet her, so she will sew you new dresses. I for one shall tell her all the sweet nothings I know, on the off-chance that she might sew me a dress as beautiful as Jealousia's was, before it became all covered with stains."

Jealousia, seeing that her scarf was once again as good as new, knew not whether she ought to treat her sister with contempt or not. Spitefulnia, however, felt a most vital urge to pronounce a few of her usual statements.

"One cannot, of course, blame the poor girl," she said with stinging envy. "Some people are by nature born base and vulgar."

"Indeed; like you, for instance," Jealousia said maliciously.

Spitefulnia pounced at her and seized her by the hair bun.

Jealousia turned around, and gave her a smack that resonated all the way to the scullery, where Little Irene was cooking the birds in red sauce, and Polycarpus was rinsing the wild greens.

Immediately there followed an outburst of screaming.

"The same as always!" muttered Little Irene.

And abandoning her stewpot to Polycarpus's care, she ran to the dining room, entering just as the Prince was holding back Jealousia firmly in one corner, while the

King, collapsed on the sofa, was restraining an enraged Spitefulnia by the skirt.

"Oh, shame, my sisters, shame!" said Little Irene ruefully. "Do not scream like this! You will wake up the entire land!"

As soon as her sisters caught sight of her, they suddenly abandoned all fighting, to ask if it had really been she who had darned their clothes—how *had* she done it?

So Little Irene took out her needles and thread, and sat on the window ledge to show them how to use them.

"Father," the Prince then said, "last night I found a letter at Faintheart's house, only I do not know how to read it, so I have brought it to you."

The King took it, put on his spectacles, and read out:

Your Excellency!

I expect no other visitor apart from Your Eminence today at my house, and so because I have no time to come myself to yours, I am leaving here this letter, so you may find it and know immediately that we, you and I both, are in the gravest danger. The Prince, who seems to be a lion cub and an eaglet too, knows that you never sold your chain of office. He knows some other things besides, which could well damage you, were you to remain here. I am making off as we speak, chain and all, to go to the King the Royal Uncle, where, as I am hoping, thanks to some information that I intend to give him regarding the lamentable condition of our State, I shall persuade him to come to my aid with his army so that I may conquer that fine piece of land that the King refused to grant me as a gift, and which lies yonder by the river. Should you wish to, come and find me.

Bring with you the diamond-studded goblets of the King, and the last remaining jewels of the Queen, which are in your cellar, and which would be worth a fair number of florins. Fear nothing, for there can be no battle without soldiers, victory is ours. Only leave at once.

Your faithful servant,

Faintheart

The King raised his eyes, and looked at his son from above his reading spectacles.

"What can this mean?" he enquired, baffled and dazed.

The Prince took a few steps around the room; he then went back to the King.

"It means, father, that this letter was intended for Cunningson. It means that Faintheart is not only a blackguard, but also a traitor, and that in a few days, a few hours, perhaps, the armies of the King our Royal Uncle could be invading our State. It also means another thing: that he appears to know things that we ourselves ignore, for instance the fact that we have no army, and that there will be no resistance at the borders."

"What nonsense and fiddlesticks!" said the King uneasily. "No army, he says! Drivel and twaddle, I say! I can throw into my uncle's kingdom thousands of soldiers, whenever and however I wish to. And a hundred ironclad fighting vessels the river shall carry southwards, at my slightest command! We have no army, he says! I shall hang the first man who dares say so again, and I'll throw his corpse to the vultures, that they may feast upon it!"

And, livid with rage, the King shoved this crown back to the top of his head, and with long strides marched twice, thrice, up and down the room.

The Prince glanced with forlorn eyes at the donkey's head, which gazed with derision at them all from above the gold-leaf cabinet, its tin crown perched impertinently between its ears.

"Father," he said at last, "call the Supreme Commander of the Army. He will give us the information we need."

The King rang the bell, and immediately Polydorus the equerry appeared before him.

"Summon the Supreme Commander of the Army at once," commanded the King, and resumed his nervous pacing up and down the room.

The equerry bowed, and made as though to leave. But at the door he stopped.

"My lord…" he muttered, "I do not know who the Supreme Commander is."

"You do not know?" cried his sovereign with rage. "You do not know?"

And changing tone:

"Hmmm… I do not know myself any more what his name is… Blast and bebother that idiot Cunningson, why did he have to go and kill himself just when I need him? He took care of everything, and knew everything like the back of his hand!… Well, then, summon my chamberlain, Cartwheeler."

Polydorus bowed deeply, and left.

A few minutes later he returned with the Lord Chamberlain.

Master Cartwheeler was short and fat, with swollen, sagging cheeks, and such an enormous belly that he could never go through a doorway or near a piece of furniture without stumbling and bumping.

"Cartwheeler," said the King imperiously, "call immediately the General-in-Chief."

"My lord," Cartwheeler replied, struggling in vain to bend at the waist in order to bow. "My lord, we have not had a General-in-Chief for these past two years."

The King almost choked with furious indignation. The blood flooded to his head, he turned a deep, dark purple.

"What are you saying?… What are you saying?" he faltered, before his voice broke, and he could not utter another word.

"My lord," Cartwheeler repeated, unperturbed, "our last General-in-Chief was Master Rogue. It has been two years now since he sold his house and went abroad, where he is known to everyone as the most prosperous banker."

"And where might he have got the florins to do that?" bellowed the King.

"A great mystery, that, my lord."

"Summon the Admiral-in-Chief, then," ordered the King nervously. And again he began to pace up and down the room.

But as he made to turn, with hands crossed, his forehead bowed and clouded, he instantly collided with the barrel-shaped belly of Cartwheeler, who had had no time to remove himself from his path.

"So what are you standing there for? Summon, I said, the Admiral-in-Chief!" he said angrily.

His equanimity intact, the Lord Chamberlain attempted once again to bow.

"We have no Admiral-in-Chief, my lord," he said calmly.

The King collapsed upon the sofa. His knees had buckled under him, his voice too was broken, and he remained there utterly devastated.

"What became of the Admiral-in-Chief?" asked the Prince.

"He is a mighty merchant abroad, my lord," answered the Lord Chamberlain. "He trades in iron."

"And how did he come upon so many florins as well?" asked the King, fuming with rage.

"He came upon them only recently."

"But by what means? Tell me that!"

"With the iron from the naval fleet."

The King received the news with a great staggering shock. He sprang up with a leap, and ran to the door.

"Mad! Mad, they are all mad! All of them!" he yelled. And seeing Polydorus the equerry at the door:

"Sound the call to arms immediately," he commanded. "Muster the troops at once, from every corner of the kingdom!"

And he rushed out running, his mantle flying behind him like the swelling sails of a ship.

The Prince followed him; far behind, panting and round as a ball, scampered the Lord Chamberlain. From the highest turret Polydorus sounded the call to arms with the great trumpet.

The King and his son ran without stopping to the barracks.

By the doorway, they found the old garrison commander, only half-awake and half-dressed, stupefied and bewildered.

He struggled to make sense of the purpose of the trumpet call, which he had not heard for so very many years.

"Where are the soldiers? Summon them all here at once!" ordered the King. The knees of the old garrison commander buckled under him, and he landed sitting squarely upon the ground.

A second time the equerry sounded the call to arms from high up on the turret. And then, all of a sudden, from the corner of the square, out of a tavern, there came a single, solitary, one-legged man, who hurried to the barracks, drew from under a mattress a rusty lance with no head, and hobbled his way to where the King and the Prince stood; pulling himself up to attention before them, he presented arms.

82

"Who is he?" asked the King.

"The army, my lord," answered the one-legged man.

"I am in no mood for pleasantries," said the King. "Do you know whom you are addressing?"

"My liege and king," replied the one-legged man, without changing his position.

"Well, then, be lost with you, before I have time to get cross. The troops will be coming out any time now, and ragamuffins such as yourself have no place in their midst."

"But I am the troops, I am the army, my lord," said the one-legged man again.

"Is he insane, or insolent?" asked the King, turning to the garrison commander, who still sat exactly where he had landed, his feet sockless inside his worn slippers. Immobile, the old man replied as though in a daze:

"He is neither insane nor insolent. He is the troops; he is the army."

"Where is the royal guard? Where are the cavalry and the lancers?" enquired the Prince quietly, thinking that perhaps the garrison commander had been struck dumb with fright.

But the old man stretched out his hand and pointed to the one-legged man.

"*There* is the guard, *there* is the army too," he replied. "I have no other troops, my lords. You may go up to the dormitories, if you wish, and see for yourselves whether I am lying or not."

And because the King and the Prince remained still, unwilling to believe, the old man continued:

"You remember the old times, my good lords. Gone are those times, nor will they ever return again."

Just then, Cartwheeler finally arrived, flushed red and sweating, hot from running.

The King pointed to the old garrison commander, who was still sitting on the ground, and with one hand made a sign to indicate that the man was not entirely right in the head.

"He is not all there," he said in a hushed tone.

"He is all there, my lord," replied the Lord Chamberlain, "and he is telling you the truth. There are no troops—"

"What is all this nonsense, for heaven's sake!" interrupted the King, who was beginning to become angry once again. "Let him summon the officers and I shall show you then where my army is."

And turning to the old man:

"Fetch at once General… General… what's his name? Never mind the name," he screamed, enraged.

"There is no general here, my lord," replied the garrison commander, trembling and shaking.

"Well, then, call the Commander of the Corps!"

"There is no Commander of the Corps!"

"Then call whomever you like, but call someone!" yelled the King, quite beside himself.

"We are all of us here, my lord!" said the old man, with a most pitiful expression on his face.

"But then the army…"

"There is no army any longer, long gone is the army, finished—you seek it in vain, my lord! There are just the two of us, my cook and myself!"

The King seized his head with both hands.

"Is it I who am going mad? Perhaps I do not understand?… You talk utter nonsense!" he burst out angrily again. "I know well that I have an army, for I pay for it every year…"

And, changing his tone:

"In fact, what do I pay for it exactly?" he asked the Lord Chamberlain.

"I do not know, my lord. You managed such accounts with the High Chancellor. I never laid eyes on them…"

"I pay… um… Well, I pay a great deal!" the King continued nervously. "And I also pay for my navy… well, an equal amount. Where is the navy? The soldiers must be on the ships! Where are the ships?"

No one knew.

With the corner of his mantle he wiped the perspiration that had formed strings of beads on his forehead.

"Let us go to the naval base," he ordered.

And with his son he hastened to the river, while farther behind, far away, tumbling at every step, followed the miserable Lord Chamberlain.

They reached the river, which ran its course, tranquil and transparent, between the green wooded riverbanks where no house could be seen, no matter how far one strained one's eye.

There were only two shabby old feluccas there, moored to the shore by a long rope, rocking away lazily on the silvery waters; a wide plank, nailed to the sides at each end, joined them together at the middle and held one next to the other.

Sprawled across the prow of one of the boats there slept a one-armed man, his mouth agape.

The King gazed up and down the river, yet he saw nothing but lush green grass, many trees, and some stones, fallen from some old derelict wall, black and begrimed by time and humidity.

"Let us go farther south," he said, and walked a few paces forward.

He found, however, no ships, no naval base.

"Would you yourself know where they are?" asked the King of Cartwheeler, who was only just then catching up with them, half-dead from the unfamiliar matinal exertion.

"I do not know, my lord, I have never been this far abroad," he replied, gasping for breath. "But maybe we could ask this sleeping bargeman."

And placing his hands in front of his mouth so as to form a cone, he cried out:

"Hey there!... Bargeman!... Wake up!..."

The one-armed man twitched his single hand ever so slightly and slowly, but did not wake up.

"Wait," said the Prince.

And, tugging at the rope, he pulled the two boats close to the riverbank.

"Ahoy there, bargeman! Hey, bargeman!" Cartwheeler cried out once more.

The one-armed man sat up and rubbed his eyes.

"What is the matter?" he asked in a sleepy voice.

"Where are the navy and the naval base?" enquired the King.

With a brisk jump, the one-armed man stood up and gave a sharp military salute.

"Present and correct!" he cried out.

"*Where are the navy and the naval base?*" asked the King again, thinking that the man had not understood him the first time.

"*Present and correct!*" repeated the one-armed man a little more loudly, without breaking off his salute.

"He does not understand!" said the King, disheartened. "My good man, can you listen to what I am saying to you? *Where are the ships and the sailors?*"

"*Present! Present and present again*," screamed the one-armed man, with such energy that the veins of his throat swelled to bursting point, while standing hard as a board he continued to present his military salute.

The Prince tried to make him understand in turn.

"We are looking for the King's ships," he explained.

"*Prrrresent!*" repeated the one-armed man. "The Royal Navy, comprising of the vessels *Fright* and *Turmoil*, present and correct! The navy of His Majesty the King present and correct!"

King Witless jumped.

"What's that?" he cried out, mortified. "What names did you say?"

"*Fright* and *Turmoil*, my dining room and bedroom. At your disposal, should you desire to visit them," said the one-armed man, with a smile that split his face from one ear to the other.

The Prince turned ashen.

"And the naval base? Where is the naval base?" he asked.

"Prrrresent!" replied again the one-armed man, indicating the blackened stones that lined the rock face all the way down to the very edge of the riverbank.

"Wait a second, now," said the King nervously, sweeping his son aside. "He does not understand, surely. Listen here, my good man, tell me where the Supreme Commander of the Army lives."

The one-armed man stretched out his hand and pointed vaguely westward.

"Abroad," he said briefly.

"And the Admiral-in-Chief... the Royal Admiral... there has to be an admiral somewhere, for heaven's sake!"

"We have nothing of the sort in this place."

"Commanders, sailors, ships, in God's name, where are all of these?"

"Present," said again the one-armed man.

And pointing proudly at his shabby old feluccas:

"Navy, present and correct."

Then, thumping his chest:

"Commander, sailor and the rest, present and correct! Look not for more, my lord, for there is no more to be found."

He picked up a plank that lay in one of his feluccas, shoved it to the bank, where he made it secure.

"Come, and be welcome in my little palace," he said with his wide smile, bowing all the way to the ground and placing his hand, fingers outstretched, onto his breast. "Your servant, my good lords!"

"Let us go home, father," said the Prince, "we have learnt all that we needed to know."

And with heads bowed low they headed for the tower.

VII

New Revelations

T HEY WALKED BACK under the scorching midday heat; when they arrived, they saw Little Irene, who was beckoning to them to come closer.

"The meal is ready," she said joyfully. "Do tell me whether or not I got the stew just right!"

The King stopped short.

"You are the one who cooked?" he asked sullenly. "We will be in a fine mess when the Queen finds out."

Little Irene's happiness vanished instantly and completely. Crestfallen, she followed her father.

The table was laid, the stew was served, the glasses and plates were at each person's appointed place.

The equerry Polycarpus put the fruit in a serving bowl, and placed it before the Queen.

"Oh! What beautiful blackberries and strawberries!" Queen Barmy said delightedly. "What King or glittering magnate could have sent these to us, I wonder?"

"You dream of nothing but Kings and rich magnates," said the King peevishly, for he was himself thinking about his ships and about the King his Royal Uncle, and Faintheart's letter—and was therefore in a most foul mood. "The great donor and benefactor is dead, my fine lady, and his son will give out no more gifts."

The Queen pulled a long face. She pushed her plate away from her and leant back on her chair with majestic disdain.

All of a sudden, however, she smelt the stew, and her appetite was rekindled.

"Game fowl! Game fowl with wilted lettuce!" she exclaimed, forgetting all her sulking and petty antics. "My favourite food! Ah, *well done* to the cook for remembering! Summon him, quick. I shall appoint him… what should I appoint him, my king?"

"It is perfectly useless to seek out titles," said the King curtly. "The cook did not prepare the food, indeed we do not have a cook at all any more, or so it would seem. It is Little Irene who got the idea in her head to replace him."

The Queen let out a scream of sheer horror: "My own daughter! My own daughter a cook!"

Her nerves failed her yet again; she rose from the table and ran to her room.

Little Irene glanced at her brother, and met his own saddened gaze. She wiped away a tear in secret, and sat at the table with a deep sigh.

There was a sudden ringing of bells a few moments later, which deafened them all.

"Run," said the King to the maids-in-waiting, "quick, the Queen sends for you."

They both rose sulkily, casting greedy glances at the stew.

"Little Irene," said the dark-haired one with sweet flattery, "do save me some, joy be to your bright little eyes!"

"For me too," echoed the blonde one.

Yet she was too bored to add anything more. She went as far as the door, let the other one go through first, then turned the other way, and sat again sluggishly at her place.

The first maid-in-waiting was back in two shakes of a lamb's tail.

"The Queen demands stew and watercress," she said, winking meaningfully at Spitefulnia. "We are not, she says, to forget the strawberries, because she craves them most awfully."

"The Queen's nerves cannot long resist the mighty temptation of food," said Spitefulnia sarcastically.

"In that, she resembles your own royal ladyship…" replied Jealousia.

Before she could finish her sentence, Spitefulnia's glass was flying across the table, striking her on the forehead.

"You witch!" screamed Jealousia.

In an instant, the table had become a riotous mess, plates and glasses were being hurled across the room, and the few remaining ones would have been smashed then too, if the Prince had not had the time to push Jealousia into her room and lock the door. He then took hold of the raging Spitefulnia and locked her in a second room.

The King, his fork uplifted in his hand, was observing the entire scene with utter complacency.

Once the two doors were shut, and the room had regained its tranquillity once again, he took a second bird onto his plate, and began to eat it.

"You are not having anything?" he asked his son, who was staring pensively at the donkey's head above the gold-leaf cabinet.

"I am thinking, father, that we must go down to Cunningson's house," replied the Prince, "search his cellar immediately, and find the things that he stole from us. We must sell these at once, so that we might, with the florins we shall get in return, arm our nation—"

"Stop! Enough is enough—I am fed up with you! Since early this morning I have dragged myself everywhere with you!" the King interrupted dispiritedly. "Leave me in peace awhile. I don't know what's got into you!"

He rose from the table and went to lie down on the sofa.

"You may go where you wish," he added more calmly, "as long as you leave me be."

And turning his back to all and sundry, he fell asleep.

From where it hung above the gold-leaf cabinet, the donkey's head was still staring at them, with its broad, sardonic grin.

In her back kitchen, however, Little Irene and the equerry Polycarpus, chatting and laughing, were rinsing and drying the glasses and the plates. This is where the Prince found them.

"Little Irene," he said, "I will be going to town. Will you come with me?"

She cast off her apron on the spot, and followed him.

"We are going to Cunningson's house," he said.

And he told her the contents of Faintheart's letter, and what great need there was for them to find immediately the stolen treasure, so they could purchase arms.

They descended the mountain and reached the town; they went straight to the High Chancellor's house. The door had been left wide open.

"This is strange!" said the Prince. "Could he have gone out last night without locking his door?"

They went inside, and into all the rooms. Yet they found nothing but some old wooden furniture. They pulled out all the drawers, and opened every cupboard, but they were all empty.

Little Irene stepped on something hard that was lying on the floor near the door. She bent down, picked it up and showed it to her brother.

"A jingle bell," she said.

The Prince took it and looked at it.

"It belongs to the jester," he replied. "You can still make out the royal crown embossed on it, even though the gilding is gone. It wouldn't be so strange if Cunningson had found it and taken it, in the hope that it too would be worth something. Now let us go to the cellar."

They went down a narrow stone staircase, and came before a small iron door.

The Prince examined the lock carefully.

"He hid his treasures well!" he said. "We shall need a blacksmith to open up such a door…"

"That won't be necessary," said Little Irene, "here is the key."

And she picked up from the ground a small, elegant key that fit the lock just right.

"It is as though he dropped it here on purpose, so we might find it more easily," she added, laughing.

"Just as he left the door ajar, so we might enter the house unhindered. It all seems too easy," muttered the Prince.

He turned the key and the door opened.

The room that the two siblings entered was small, with a low ceiling and no windows.

There was a lantern still burning on the ground, and its flickering flame lit up the four bare stone walls.

Beside the lantern, there was an empty wooden chest, its lid gaping wide open.

The Prince looked around him.

Lying in a corner on the floor, there was something white against the darkness. He lifted it up to the light of the lantern and examined it.

It was a small baton, its gilding tarnished, with a doll's head at one end and trimmed with ribbons and jingle bells.

"What have you found?" asked Little Irene.

"The thief's signature," replied the Prince. "In other words, the jester's sceptre. We have come too late, Little Irene! The treasure is lost!"

"What are you saying!" cried his sister.

"I am saying," answered the Prince, pointing to the plaything he had found, "that this explains the open door, the jingle bell on the floor, the little key by the cellar door, the unextinguished lantern, and the empty cellar. It also explains to us the jester's presence by Cunningson's corpse. The dwarf was no fool; on the contrary, he must have either suspected or known about the existence of the treasure in the High Chancellor's cellar, and, first thing in the morning, when we were going out unsuspecting to find food, he himself was after a different sort of bounty. He was going down the precipice to find the key, exactly where he knew he would find it, namely inside the dead man's shirt…"

Little Irene stared dismally at the jester's sceptre.

"So what now?" she asked.

"Now we must go and ask whether anyone has seen him, and which way he was headed. I do not believe it would be possible for me to catch up with him. But I would like to try."

They locked up the cellar and went out.

Across the street from the house, by the door of a derelict grocer's shop, there stood a young boy, beggarly looking and pale; he was munching away at a small chunk of hard black bread.

The Prince went up to him and asked if he worked there.

"Yes!" said the boy. "This is my uncle's place, and when he is at the tavern I keep shop for him."

"Tell me," said the Prince, "do you know, perhaps, if the King's jester passed this way earlier this morning?"

"That he did! He came to the house of His Excellency Master Cunningson."

"Did you see him leave the house? Was he carrying anything?"

"Yes! He had a haversack slung over his shoulder."

"You did not ask him what was in it?"

"Who, me? I would not dare! He's been to Master Cunningson's several times in the past, laden with things, but he always got so angry if anyone asked him what was in his sack. How could I ask! He is nasty and sneaky."

"And where did he go?" asked the Prince.

"He headed towards the vale. He was in a hurry, running fast." Brother and sister thanked him and took their leave.

"So, that's that, he was Cunningson's accomplice," said the Prince. "He must have been the one who carried the plunder to him, stealing a few items at a time from the palace."

"Do you think we may be able to catch up with him?" asked Little Irene.

"Who knows?"

They hurried on towards the vale.

"And yet, luck is not on our side," said Little Irene sorrowfully. "If only we had arrived a little earlier, we would have found the treasure!"

"I see no place for either luck or misfortune in all that has happened," answered the Prince. "Luck is on the side of the man who can steer his ship out of a storm. If I have lost the treasure, it is my own fault, and no one else's... And do you know what I am thinking, Little Irene?" he continued, disheartened. "That I shall never achieve my purpose, because I do not know how to read and write! Last night, when I found Faintheart's letter, if I had known how to read, I would have gone after him at once, perhaps I might have caught him. And then I would have stopped him from going over to our enemies to betray us. Had I been able to read, I would have come immediately to Cunningson's house, broken down the door of the cellar and found the treasure, which is so vital to us, if we are to reassemble our army once again and buy weapons for its soldiers. Then, I could have still had time. Whereas today, when father finally read the letter, it was too late! Faintheart was far away, the cellar empty. And by now, Faintheart will have arrived at the kingdom of the King our Royal Uncle, and will have already betrayed us. And who knows what storms will fall upon our long-suffering, miserable land, storms I might have averted, *if only I had known how to read and write!*..."

Little Irene threw her arms around his neck.

"Do not talk like this! Do not be so distressed!" she said, with tears in her eyes. "It is no fault of yours that you do not know how to read and write!"

"Until this moment," the Prince went on, "I had never felt the need to learn anything. I would spend my days on the terrace, gazing at the sky and the valley, or going down the slope to shoot targets with my sling, my only concern being how to escape the eternal squabbles and the petty miseries of the palace… Now, however, since I came down from our mountain and have been amongst our people, I see, feel the need to learn… And I shall learn," he went on with fervour. "I shall go to the schoolmaster, I shall toil day and night, and I shall learn! Otherwise I will never be able to accomplish my purpose."

Brother and sister walked on thus for some while.

Loneliness pervaded everything. Not a single soul did they meet, neither in the fields, nor in the woods, to ask whither the jester had gone.

As they came out of the forest, they went past a small, solitary house. Its owner sat by the doorway, his head bandaged, smoking his pipe.

The Prince recognized him, and stopped to bid him good morning.

"How is your head, Miserlix?"

The man rose from his chair, grasped the boy's hand and kissed it.

"May God keep you well, my good lad," he said, choking with emotion. "I shall never forget the debt I owe you."

And noticing Little Irene, he asked:

"Is the young lass your sister?"

"Yes!"

"Come, be welcome in my poor home, sit down and rest."

"I do not have time to stop," said the Prince. "I am chasing a man who runs before me; he has a good head start, and I must catch up with him at all costs."

"If you are chasing someone the likes of you and me, then mayhap you could gain on him. But if you are running after some palace courtier, you would need to have the jester's horse to catch him."

"A horse? The jester has a horse? Where did you see him?"

"He went past this way at daybreak. He was making the horse gallop as if it had been stung by the devil himself…"

"But how came he by the horse?" asked the Prince.

Miserlix laughed.

"Those palace men come by anything they want, don't you worry," he said. "Faintheart was on horseback too, when he went past this way yesterday, under cover of night."

"They took the same road?"

"Yes! And as he passed by this morning, the dwarf shouted to me, asking whether I had any greetings to send to Master Faintheart, because he would be seeing him again, as he said, very soon." And looking keenly at the Prince, who stood crestfallen and with his arms crossed: "Don't let it break your heart, my lad," he went on. "Do come inside, you and your sister. You chase him in vain—you will never catch up with him now!"

Once inside, Miserlix's daughter brewed coffee, served it in iron cups, and placed these before them on an iron tray.

The Prince noticed that all the furnishings were also made of iron, and asked why.

"And how would it be otherwise? Mine is the blacksmith's craft, my lad," replied Miserlix. "Once upon a time, I was the one who forged all the swords, arrow tips and suits of armour in the kingdom, it was I who would clad the mighty ships with iron, ships which filled the river and spread terror to every neighbour. But the good years are now gone, the ships are lost, as are the weapons, and the palace does not order new ones; my hands hang worthless, useless. What iron was left in my storehouse I used to make furniture, just so I would have something to busy myself with, and not sit around doing nothing. I have no iron left, however. And so, here I sit, idling away the time, smoking my pipe, while my daughter sells her needlework to bring some bread into the house. Everything has been turned upside down, my lad!"

The Prince's eyes flashed with the new hopes that were being born in his heart.

"And long ago, at the time when the palace still commissioned swords, where did you buy the iron?"

"I did not buy it. The palace provided me with it."

"And where did the palace get it from?"

"Ah, my boy, those were the days when everyone prospered here. Many were the young men and the families who owed their livelihood to the State mines and quarries. You could see them going down the pits every day, like armies of ants, extracting the stones, and as many more would be busy in the workshops, where they would separate the ore from the rock. I was then managing one hundred hard-working craftsmen, we earned our bread lavishly, and there wasn't a soul left without his beef stew or his roast chicken on a Sunday. Those days are gone and vanished, never to return!" said Miserlix with a sigh.

"And why couldn't the good days come back, I wonder?" said the Prince eagerly. "Why might not the work begin anew, with miners extracting iron, so you could make again arrow tips and spearheads?"

Miserlix smiled.

"And who would be paying for all the hard-toiling labourers? The King is up to his ears in debt. He does not even have food to eat."

The Prince bowed his head at this, heavy as lead with dark sadness. He needed florins! Where *could* he find florins?

He remembered the lost treasure, and his heart felt quashed, strangled by an iron grip. He rose to take his leave of Miserlix and his daughter.

"Come," he said to Little Irene. "Let us go to the schoolmaster straight away." But they had no time to go to his house, for they met him on their way.

"Good greetings to you, my children," said the schoolmaster, recognizing the two siblings. "Where are you going?"

"I was coming to find you," said the Prince. "I have a favour to ask, and I was heading towards your house."

"What a pity!" said the schoolmaster. "I was just now going to town, to see my brother who lives there. Could you perhaps explain while we walk?"

"Why not? I too must go back to the capital with my sister, so we can talk on the way there. I have a proposition for you. I want to learn how to read and write. Will you teach me?"

"Well done! But how much will you pay me? You know I am a poor man. I cannot teach for nothing—"

"I have no money to give you, nor anything else of value," interrupted the Prince, "but I propose the following arrangement. You only have some wild greens to live on, which the children cultivate on your behalf—"

"Not wild greens, just tubers," interrupted the schoolmaster. "I grow nothing but carrots, onions and the like now, plants whose yield cannot be seen. Otherwise, all is stolen from me."

"Well then. What I propose is to bring you a fowl or a hare or a rabbit or any other game I might kill for every lesson you give me. Do you accept?"

"Do I? And how!" said the schoolmaster, overjoyed. "So many years has it been since I last ate meat that I have near forgotten what it tastes like."

They were walking through the woods.

The schoolmaster took a thick dry branch, cut it and trimmed it into small squares, and scratched on each a letter of the alphabet. Then he sat down at the root of a tree, and spread them before him.

"Come," he said, "and I shall first teach you the letters and the sounds."

The schoolmaster had good patience, and the students were eager and keen to learn. And so, when the sun set, the three of them were still sitting beneath the tree, shuffling the wooden squares and sorting them out again, to form syllables and words.

"This is good," said the schoolmaster. "If we always work as well as we did today, you shall learn even more things than I know myself. Soon I shall give you books too, so you may read on you own."

They took again the way to the capital. As they walked, they talked of many things.

"Had you passed this way during the days of Prudentius I, it would have seemed to you that the entire land was one great, busy factory," said the schoolmaster.

"What did everyone do then?" asked the Prince.

"They built ships," answered the schoolmaster. "And the master builder was my brother. They felled the trees, and carried them down to the river, building there the royal ships, which were then taken to the naval base."

"And where is your brother now?" asked the Prince fervently.

"He lives in the capital: that is where I am going tonight. But the poor man barely makes ends meet, always living from hand to mouth. If he has one unlucky turn, one day of sickness, he will lose his bread."

"What is his name?"

"Illstar the master builder, to distinguish him from myself, whom they call Illstar the schoolmaster."

"I would very much like to meet him," said the Prince.

"And why not? Instead of going all the way to the School of the State, come tomorrow to his house to have your lesson. If you come early, you will find me there."

"Very well, then, I will come."

In front of the door of the master builder's house, the schoolmaster bid them goodbye, and the Prince went up the mountain slope with Little Irene.

It was late by the time they reached the palace. Everyone was asleep.

Polycarpus alone had anxiously stayed up for them, venturing outside to see if they were approaching, then again going inside, back to the bench where Polydorus lay asleep, to tell him about his worries, which the sleeping man never heard at all.

"I have saved up some food for you, my lady, and also for His Highness, your brother," he said happily to Little Irene when he saw her. "Go into the dining hall, your young Highness, I have the table all laid out properly."

Polydorus, however, had been awakened by the voices and was already lighting a torch so they could see their way to the dining hall. He could not light a lantern, for there were no wax tapers or even a tallow candle in the palace any more. So they stuck the torch into a clay pitcher, and by its light brother and sister sat down to eat.

The next day, first thing in the morning, they went once more to the woods, where the Prince killed wildfowl and rabbits, while Little Irene collected eggs from birds' nests, and picked fruit, and gathered wild greens.

When they returned, still no one was awake. Only Polycarpus was up, getting the back kitchen ready once more for Little Irene.

The Prince took from the pile the schoolmaster's share, and bid Little Irene farewell.

"I shan't be long," he said. "The master builder's house is very near the foot of the mountain, and I will be back as soon as I have finished my lesson."

He found the schoolmaster and his brother sitting inside the glassed-in porch of the house, eating bread and olives.

"Welcome, my good lad," said the schoolmaster, and introduced his brother to the Prince.

The Prince immediately entered into a deep discussion with the master builder, asking him a myriad questions about the way he used to build ships in the past, and the master builder remembered with sadness and with longing the earlier years of his life, relating with tears in his eyes how deeply stirred he had been every time that he would see on the river some new ship, built by his own hands.

"Do you still have the urge to build ships?" asked the Prince. The master builder smiled cynically.

"You must not jest about such things," he said. "Such pleasantries leave a bitter aftertaste."

"Yet… and yet, if there might be someone… the King, let us say… and he were to commission new ships, would you build them?"

"The King will not commission them, rest assured," said the master builder scornfully. "His entire life the King never thought of anything but his own comfort and peace of mind. Now it is too late for him to wake up. Thanks to his High Chancellors, his Supreme Commanders of the Army, his Commanders of the Fleet and their fine company, he does not even have food to eat any more."

"What did the Supreme Commander of the Army do, exactly, do you know?" asked the Prince.

"You ask about Master Rogue? As though there were a man alive who did not know! He did the same as every other palace courtier. He had absolute control over the army warehouses, and he emptied them all. Once he had sold the armaments, the tents and the uniforms, he had amassed a considerable fortune and he went with it abroad, whilst his royal master never even suspected his absence. Even the stones know what I am telling you. It is a secret well known to everyone in the land! The King is the only one who never seems to hear of any of these things," added the master builder.

"Is it really fair to put the blame on the King," said the Prince, turning his face away, pretending to be looking at the street, but in truth trying to conceal the bright scarlet flush on his face. "How could it be the King's fault, if he has only thieves and scoundrels in his entourage?"

"He ought to have taken care to know the members of his staff before entrusting them with the best interests of the State," said the master builder, angry and indignant. "And when they turned out to be scoundrels, he ought to have punished them. But when did he ever care about anything? We are always plagued by so-called feelings of good charity! How could you punish a thief, or a traitor, or any other irresponsible and unscrupulous man? 'The poor wretch,' they tell you. 'Why should his life be ruined? Many others do far, far worse!' And so on and so forth. And it is only the honest men who cannot earn their bread in this land!"

The Prince interrupted him—so as not to hear more against his father.

"Why are there people running in the street?" he asked, pointing to two or three peasants, who were running hurriedly with their wives towards the mountain.

The two Illstars peered out of the window.

"It must be some brawl again," said the master builder quietly. "We here are used to such goings-on; they no longer make an impression on us."

"Do you frequently have brawls?" asked the Prince.

"Of course we do; ever since state justice became lax and then was done away with altogether, everyone seeks to defend his right on his own, and seeks to take vengeance on the man who wronged him, or whom he only believes to have wronged him. And so every day there is violent brawling in the capital and in the villages. Quite often there are murders too. Yet the Law will take no notice! There is not a single policeman to be found anywhere any more!"

The Prince listened, and his soul became more and more distraught on account of the miseries plaguing his land. Whatever he might have to say, the conversation always evolved into a long, grievous complaint.

"And the lesson, then?" asked the schoolmaster, interrupting their talk. "What, you bring me such a scrumptious little rabbit, and you would not learn anything further?"

The Prince took his chips of wood out of his pocket and the lesson began.

"If you can learn as fast every day," the schoolmaster said, pleased, "I shall soon give you the books I promised, for you to read them on your own."

Without warning, the door was suddenly thrown open, and the equerry Polydorus entered, panting and covered in dust.

"My lord," he said, and his voice was trembling, "the King asks you to come at once. Bad tidings have come. His Majesty is at a loss, he weeps and calls for you—the Princess has sent me to ask you to come immediately."

"My *lord*?!" cried the schoolmaster in a daze.

The master builder started.

"My *lord*?!" he repeated in turn.

The Prince had risen from his seat. His face was deathly pale.

"The King our Royal Uncle…" he muttered.

"Who *are* you?! *Who* are you?!" shouted the master builder, who remembered petrified the words he had uttered earlier.

"I am the King's son," said the Prince, stretching out his hand to him. "And now it is I who command you to stop whatever you are doing, and build a new fleet. And if I have no florins to give you, even if many years must pass before I can pay you, again do not stop, only work hard, until the river is swarming again with ships. The time has come for us all to make sacrifices. Forget your own little self and your personal interest, work only for the common good of the land. Our homeland asks this, and I shall myself set the example for all of you."

The master builder fell upon his knees, seized the boy's hand and kissed it.

"I *shall* rebuild the fleet," he said fervently, "and I shall work until all my strength is gone."

The Prince then went out, his soul in turmoil. Polydorus followed him. Those last words had electrified him and his heart was swelling with love and admiration for his new lord, for the young man who had uttered them.

VIII

The King's Crown

T HE KING was pacing up and down with nervous, uneven strides, while fat tears trickled down his fleshy, rosy cheeks.

When he saw his son, he let out a cry:

"My boy! The storm is upon us!"

At that, he collapsed on a chair, hiding his face in his hands and crying with heavy sobs.

By his side, placid and indifferent, stood Master Cartwheeler, his arms resting crossed upon his belly, awaiting the orders of his lord with his usual impassivity.

The Prince approached the King.

"Father," he said, trying to conceal the emotional whirlwind in his heart, "father, weep not. We have need of all our courage and all our strength. Tell me, what is the matter? I know nothing yet!"

The King beckoned to the Lord Chamberlain to relate the news.

"A few hours ago terrified peasants came to the palace,"

Master Cartwheeler began, "and they told us that the enemy had crossed the borders and was invading our kingdom—"

"What enemy is that?" interrupted the Prince.

"The King your Royal Uncle," replied Master Cartwheeler.

"I expected this to happen sooner or later. Speak further."

"…and the enemies have now halted their advance, as though afraid to proceed. With them is also Faintheart the Judge, who is leading them, and is trying to convince them that the road is clear, that they can go as far as the river. They are frightened, however, and for the time being they have set up camp instead. They have sent some scouts ahead towards the river, to make sure that the area is truly free, so that they may then immediately move in and occupy the entire valley. These are the tidings," added Master Cartwheeler, resuming his usual impassivity.

The King raised himself up a little.

"Now do you understand, my son? You have heard it all?" he said, weary and spent.

"I have heard. And now, father, the time has come to act. What do you advise?"

"It is I who must ask you that question, my son. What advice do *you* have? I have already told you that in the future you and I shall rule together."

"Well, then, father, and my king, my advice is that I should leave immediately and go from one end of the kingdom to the other, to rouse every youth or old man, or boy even, who may bear a lance or hold a sword, and bring them here, so we may give them any piece of iron which may be found in our towns and villages; then send them at once across the river, where I will lead them against the enemy. I also advise one other thing. Your crown, father: you must give it now to be sold abroad."

Aghast, the King seized his crown with his two hands.

"No, my son, do not take it away from me," he cried out, genuinely distressed. "Do not sell it! *I want it!*"

"It is most necessary, father," insisted the Prince. "Our first need is for florins, and your crown is the only thing of value left in the palace. The time has come when all of us must make sacrifices. Let this one be yours. Give me the crown, father, I ask it in the name of our homeland."

The King was now sobbing heavily.

"But I, how *can* I be left without my crown?" he said. "You deprive me of my power and authority by taking away the insignia of my office!"

"On the contrary, I give them and restore them back to you," replied the Prince. "By giving away your crown so that arms may be bought, you acquire the right to ask for sacrifices from those who shall use these arms to liberate our land. Hand me your crown, father, I beg you on my knees, give it to me!"

The King removed his golden crown; and, turning his face away in order to hide the tears that ran fast down his cheeks, he delivered it into the hands of his kneeling son.

The Prince sprang briskly to his feet.

"And now," he cried out, "now I seek a valiant man—someone who will make every sacrifice of himself, will cross our country's border as fast as lightning, sell it, and bring me back its worth in florins."

From the door where he stood, Polydorus had watched the entire scene, his heart bursting with emotion. His earlier excitement had now turned into unbridled fervour.

He took a step forward and fell on his knees before the Prince.

"As an inestimable favour, I ask you, my lord, to entrust the crown to me," he said, "and allow me to go abroad, sell it, and bring back its value in florins, or lose my life in the attempt."

"Go, then," said the Prince, "fly away and come back swiftly! And may God be with you!"

Polydorus took the crown, kissed the hand that handed it to him, and left the palace running.

Straight to the river he headed, the precious crown hidden away in the folds of his surcoat; he ran without halting to the place where the two shabby old feluccas were moored, still joined by the plank nailed across their middle.

"Fellow countryman!" he cried out. "Ahoy!… Fellow countryman!…"

The one-armed man, who was enjoying the morning sunshine flat on his back, his one arm under his head, stood up.

"Present and correct!" he cried out.

"What do you ask to ferry me across?" asked Polydorus. "Only do not ask me for florins, for I have none."

"What do you want to go across for?" asked the one-armed man.

"Secret mission of the State," replied the equerry.

Unhurriedly, the one-armed man took his long punt pole and, thrusting it all the way to the riverbed, he pushed his feluccas to the bank.

"Get in," he said, and the equerry jumped into the boat. "Where to?"

"The opposite bank. Put me ashore wherever you want, or wherever you can, only get me across the river fast."

The one-armed man untied the rope, took again his punt pole and dug it into the riverbed; walking slowly from stern to starboard and pushing on his punt pole, he manoeuvred his boats away from the bank.

"And you go far?" he asked.

"Yes, very far!"

The one-armed man reached the end of the felucca he stood in, and came back to the stern, trailing his punt pole behind him. He thrust it into the water again, and resumed his stroll to starboard.

"You are here to serve the whim of the State, then, so to speak, which is to say the whimsy of Sire Witless? Just so you can test how well they prick those lances of the King our Royal Uncle? Or don't you know, mayhap, that our Very Royal Uncle has disembarked himself on our land, without even asking our leave?"

"I do know it," replied Polydorus calmly.

"And knowing that, you do not turn to go back?" asked

the one-armed man in a lilting, sing-song voice, always continuing his stroll. "You are quite something, aren't you, my good lad?"

For some time neither of them spoke.

The one-armed man dragged his punt pole once again from the water, and returned to the stern.

"And what might he be paying you, his lordship, to make you willing to go and catch your death over yonder?" he asked.

"I did not ask for payment."

"Is that so, now? You have certainly fallen from a strange star, my lad. And you go just like that, you say? For the sake of those black eyes of Sire Witless?"

"No, rather for the brown ones of his son."

"Is that so? Is that so, indeed?" said the one-armed man, and his broad smile split his face from ear to ear.

It was some time before they spoke again. The one-armed man continued to push his feluccas onwards.

"And so then, how did he kindle such a fire in you, this fine son of his?" he asked after a while.

"Just so! With what he said. I heard him… I saw him…" replied the equerry. "And he shook me all over, he seized my whole being, and made me his. And were he to say to me, 'Throw yourself into the fire,' I should throw myself into the fire."

"And now he has told you, 'Throw yourself at the lances', and you are throwing yourself at the lances," said the one-armed man in his customary imperturbable manner.

"Yes," Polydorus replied simply.

They did not speak again until they had reached the opposite side, and had drawn the boats nearer to the shore.

The equerry leapt out and onto the dry land. "So what do you ask, then, for your trouble?" he asked.

"Your good love," replied the one-armed man, pulling his punt pole back up again.

"At least tell me your name. I do not want to forget you."

"Onearm."

"Thank you."

The equerry turned to go.

"Ahoy, there, countryman, and what's yours?" cried the one-armed man.

"What's mine what?"

"Your name!"

"Polydorus."

"All right, then. Listen to one more thing. When you return… for you shall return, of course…"

"Yes!"

"You will find me, in that case, standing before you if you go to the right place; otherwise"—and with his hand he made the gesture of a dive—"*splosh*, into the river."

The equerry, who had moved away, approached again.

"Which is the right place?"

"Not here, of course!" said the one-armed man. "For by that time, our guests will have arrived as well, and your body would have as many holes as a colander before you ever reached *Fright* and *Turmoil*. You will find me,

however"—and with his hand he pointed up the river—
"there, where the Fool's Eddy meets the river."

"But that's a terrible, nasty spot, how will you go there?
The currents of the eddy are far too strong," said Polydorus.

"And that's just why our guests will never think of coming
there to greet us," replied the one-armed man quietly, and
with one thrust he pushed his boats away. "Godspeed to
you, countryman!"

"Godspeed to you too!"

Shifting his punt pole with slow, steady steps, the one-
armed man once again headed for the opposite bank,
singing softly:

> *Five years have I wandered,*
> *Five years have I wandered,*
> *On the mountains, the mountains,*
> *Oh, dear love of mine, on the mountains.*

IX

Where Fate Has Seen Fit to Place Us…

IN THE MEANTIME, the Prince had asked for the Great Ledger of the Royal Army, where all the officers and soldiers were registered.

The King turned to the Lord Chamberlain.

"Fetch it at once," he commanded.

The Lord Chamberlain left the dining hall unhurriedly, and went to the back kitchen, where Polycarpus was wiping a serving platter with exemplary zeal for Little Irene, who was herself engaged in browning the game.

"Fetch it at once," commanded Master Cartwheeler.

"Fetch what at once?" asked the equerry.

"The ledger with the lists for the Royal Army."

"Where is it?"

"I know no more than you do. Find it and get it."

The equerry looked at Little Irene with baffled eyes.

"Who is asking for it?" asked Little Irene.

"His Highness your brother, Your Royal Ladyship," replied the Lord Chamberlain.

"Oh, Polycarpus! You simply *must* find it!" pleaded Little Irene.

Her words had hardly been spoken before Polycarpus had abandoned serving platter and dishcloth, and was dashing off to the cellar.

He looked closely into everything, ferreted about, turned upside down every single thing there was to be found in the cellar; he discovered nothing. Running like mad, and covered with dust, he scurried up to the first floor, opened every cupboard, drawer, chest and hamper there was in the palace tower, and still he found nothing. Like a cat, he crawled up the steep ladder leading to the attic, and there, at long last, after rummaging in every corner, having opened every storeroom, having plunged almost bodily into every old chest and coffer that lay there dilapidated, each a mouldy old relic eaten by woodworm and maggots, he pulled out, from under a pile of old, yellowed and crumpled papers, a tattered, oblong book, its covers half-devoured by mice, and so impregnated with dust that the gilded lettering on the jacket could barely be deciphered any longer.

He loaded it onto his back, and triumphantly he took it down to the dining hall, where the King and the Prince were still discussing things, while a cross-armed Master Cartwheeler yearned for them to conclude their talk, so that he might have leave to return home (where he knew that a mouth-watering mash of garlic and walnuts awaited him).

The equerry placed the book on the table.

"What is this miserable rag?" asked the Prince.

"I do not know," said the equerry, "but it is the only book in the palace."

The King opened it and leafed through it.

"Of course, this is it," he said. "I can see both names and titles."

And he began to read at random:

"Axer, commander of the corps; Terrorman, general; Fearless, marshal; Thunderson, centurion."

He turned to the Lord Chamberlain, and ordered:

"Summon at once General Terrorman!"

Master Cartwheeler strove hard to bow.

"He is dead, my lord, he's been dead and gone eight years now."

"Ah… Hmm…" grunted the King. "Then summon Axer, Commander of the Corps."

"Passed away, my lord, twelve years ago."

"Then surely this must be his son. Summon his son," ordered the King nervously.

"His son was not in the army, my lord. He spent all his money, and then went into service with Master Rogue, the Supreme Commander of the Army; he too has left to go abroad."

"So why on earth have you brought me this age-old register, which lists only the names of dead men!" the King broke out peevishly.

He turned over some more pages towards the end.

"Ah, here are some more entries," he said, pleased with himself. "Here are also the names of soldiers. Cuckoo,

Cuckoobird, Cuckoochick, Cuckooclock, Cuckoonest, Cuckooson… Here are soldiers aplenty! Who says I have no army?"

And turning to the equerry Polycarpus:

"Command someone to go at once and summon… and summon all of these soldiers," he ordered.

But Polycarpus just stood, fixed to the ground, his mouth agape.

"Who is to go? And where?" he asked, befuddled.

"No! No!" said the Prince. "If it is at all possible to find them, we shall find them ourselves. Let us go to town, father."

"Now?" protested the King. "But we are just about to eat lunch! It is noon!"

"We shall eat more heartily later," replied the Prince.

And so the King followed him, sulking and muttering, while Master Cartwheeler was slipping away quietly, to go to his mash of walnuts and garlic.

In front of the barracks, they found the one-legged man, who was eating water-soaked broad beans with great relish.

As he saw them he stood up erect and, holding his wooden porringer, he saluted in military fashion.

"Go and fetch the garrison commander," ordered the King.

"He is bedridden with the snuffles, drinking infusions of lime-flowers," replied the one-legged man with telegraphic brevity.

"Listen here," said the Prince slowly, "do you know where I might find the soldiers who are on the army lists?"

"There are no soldiers."

"Where is Cuckoo?" asked again the Prince.

"Apprentice to the cobbler," the one-legged man replied hastily.

"What's that you say?" the King asked crossly. "With whose permission did he leave the barracks to become an apprentice? And Cuckoobird…"

"Undercook to Cuckoochick, who killed Cuckooclock in order to take from him the purse he had found in Cuckooson's shooting knapsack, the man who won three five-florin coins at the tavern; he has since left to go abroad," came the reply of the one-legged man, all in a single breath.

The King pulled at the few hairs on his head, and took flight towards the mountain.

The Prince continued his examination with blackened heart.

"And the other soldiers, where are they?"

"They are not," replied the one-legged man.

"But what became of them?"

"Nothing became of them, for they were not."

"Since when has the army ceased to exist?" asked the Prince without losing patience.

"It never ceased," answered proudly the one-legged man. "The army is me, and as the army shall I die."

The Prince understood that he was wasting his time. With head bowed low, with heart heavy as lead, he headed for Miserlix's house.

He did not know where to go. He knew no one in town of whom he might seek counsel, or help. And yet he had to find men and arms at once!

"The King paid for an army," he thought bitterly to himself, "and the soldiers became cooks, or undercooks, or thieves and cut-throats. And the florins found their way into the pockets of the numerous Cunningsons, and the army's supreme commanders sold the weapons, the chiefs of the royal fleet ransacked the naval base and dismantled the navy's ships to steal a few fistfuls of iron!"

He made every effort to understand and somehow explain the cause of all this wickedness.

He recalled the words of the master builder regarding the brawls and acts of retaliation taking place everywhere, in the villages and in the cities. He remembered the schoolmaster's words too, that there were times when it was necessary for one to be truly heroic in order to do one's duty.

Was there then no one amongst his people who had the dignity to do his duty heroically?

He could not help remembering the thefts and the villainies, petty or significant, that he witnessed everywhere, and he thought: "Is it then only in times of happiness that my people will be honourable and honest?"

Black despair seized him. He went into the woods, wandered and lost himself amidst the thick trees, and lay down on the cool grass, closing his eyes with great weariness.

"Is it worth it, putting up a fight for such people, to ache for such a land?" he murmured to himself.

"*Yes!*" said a female voice softly. "*It's worth it.*"

He opened his eyes and lifted his head, startled.

Before him stood Knowledge.

"How did *you* get here?" he asked her.

"You no longer came to my hut, and I knew that you were alone. I imagined you feeling dejected and discouraged, and I came to see you. I saw you from the road entering the woods, and I followed you. Yes, it's worth struggling for your country."

The Prince hid his face away in his hands.

"If *only you knew* what sort of people they were!" he said wearily.

"Well then, do you want to become yourself like them?"

"What do you mean?" he asked.

"I mean that you scorn these people who are your people, because they are thieves or cowards, or simply because they do not have life enough to fight against misery and the general lethargy. So then, do you want to become like them, forsake the state at the first sign of difficulty, abandon your post, show yourself a coward in the face of toil and responsibility? Your people are like all others, neither better nor worse. They need, however, governance. Could it be perhaps that it is *you yourself* who are not strong enough to be a leader?"

Knowledge gazed at him, her eyes thoughtful.

"Where fate has seen fit to place us," she went on, "there must we stay. Fate chose for you the place of a leader. In your place you must stay, and, if need be, there die with dignity and pride. And then, but only then, shall you stand higher than those you scorn. But to leave? Never that, no! That would be desertion!"

The Prince felt a shock run through him.

"I shall stay," he said with vehement yearning. "I shall work! Yes, I shall save them, even if they themselves don't want to be saved. My land, I shall make it great again, I shall give it back life, or I shall perish with it. Farewell, Knowledge, and thank you for the courage that your words have stirred up inside me."

And with great strides he left the woods, without once looking behind him.

X

At the Tavern

H E RAN STRAIGHT to Miserlix's house and found him at the table with his daughter. When they saw him, they both rose to their feet.

"Sit and catch your breath, you look tired," said Miserlix, offering him an iron stool. "Have you eaten?"

"I am not hungry," replied the Prince.

"Please, accept our poor fare," pleaded Miserlix.

And so the Prince sat at their table so as not to hurt his feelings, and the girl fetched him an iron plate.

"Miserlix," he then said, not wasting any words, "I am the King's son, and I have come to ask you a favour."

Miserlix sprang up from his seat.

"The King's son?" he exclaimed.

"The Prince!" murmured the girl.

And both fell on their knees, stunned and bewildered.

"No, no, please, do not take it so," said the Prince, helping them to rise, "I did not say this to frighten you, but to ask rather for your help. Miserlix, have you heard the evil tidings? The King our Royal Uncle has crossed the border and is advancing towards the river."

"Heaven help us!" cried the girl.

Miserlix grasped his head.

"So, then, the end has come at last," he grunted.

"No, the end has not come!" the Prince said with fervour. "As long as we all wish it, we can send the enemy away."

"But how?" asked Miserlix dispiritedly. "You have no weapons, no soldiers—"

"This is why I have come to you," interrupted the Prince. "You will make me the weapons and I shall raise the soldiers, only tell me where all the men of the land are hiding. For I have not seen a single one, either in the fields or on the roads."

Miserlix laughed a dry, bitter laugh.

"If you were to go to the tavern," he said, "you would find all of them there together."

"I shall go then to the tavern. You, however—you must not waste an instant. Forge weapons for me."

"But what with, what with?!" said Miserlix in despair. "I do not even have a pound of iron left any more!"

The Prince cast a meaningful silent glance at the iron furniture around him.

Miserlix understood the hint, and smiled.

"You want me to spoil good work that was completed long ago?" he said sadly.

"And why not, *if there is need?*" answered the Prince with burning fervour.

Seeing, however, the wretchedness on Miserlix's face, he rose up hastily:

"It would have been your duty to your King and to your country to do so, and you would have fulfilled it, no matter what it cost you personally. Yet there is no need to spoil work that has been already finished. Show me where the mines are, tell me how to extract the ore, and I shall get you at once as much iron as you desire!"

Miserlix was electrified.

"You could awaken a man long dead with that soul of yours, you could!" he said with passion. "Yours is my furniture, yours too is my life!"

And seizing hold of two pickaxes, he went outside.

"Take the handcart, a coil of cable and the miner's lamp, and follow us!" he called out to his daughter.

With long strides he headed with the Prince towards the mines, while behind them followed the girl with the handcart.

On their way they met a pale, scrawny boy, who stretched out his hand to them when he saw them.

"Why are you begging?" asked the Prince.

"I have no bread," replied the boy.

"Then come with us. I have no money to give you, but if you work, I shall give you food to quell your hunger."

So the boy followed them. They reached the pits.

"Tie the rope around my waist," said the Prince. "I shall go down myself."

He took the pickaxe, secured the lantern to his belt, and Miserlix lowered him down the shaft.

When he reached the pit bottom, he saw that there was no need to dig for ore. There were numerous loose piles of rocks already mined, even two or three baskets already filled and left lying around.

The Prince called to Miserlix to lower down the little errand boy, and together they dragged one of these baskets to the opening of the shaft, tied it up with the cable, and told Miserlix to lift it up, and to lower it down again after emptying it.

"And now, my boy, you are to do yourself as I have done," the Prince said, after they had filled several baskets in this manner. "And when your work is finished, come, and I shall give you food."

Then the Prince attached once again the rope around his waist, and went up the shaft.

He found Miserlix hacking at the ore stones with his pickaxe, separating the metal from the raw earth, and piling it in the handcart.

"Now go back home," he said to his daughter. "Unload there the metal, and bring me back the handcart."

And he asked the Prince:

"You leave us, my lord?"

"Yes! I shall go to the tavern. Time flies, and I must gather together the soldiers who are to fight with the swords and spears that you will make for me," the Prince replied.

The Prince and Miserlix's daughter set off together. On the way, they talked.

"You hope in vain that you could ever fight against your enemies, my lord," said the girl sorrowfully. "You have no soldiers."

"I shall find them," replied the Prince. "This is why I am going to the tavern."

"They will never follow you, they don't care any more about this land, and whether it should perish; they only have two thoughts in their heads, gaming and wine. But even if they were to follow you, how could my father ever manage to forge so many weapons on his own? And furthermore, my father is a blacksmith: he can make arrow tips and spearheads, but not arrow shafts and lances. He does not work with wood."

"What you say is right," replied the Prince. "But what happened to all the craftsmen who used to work for your father in the past?"

"Some have left, some have changed trades. The best one amongst them, his brother, opened his own smithy. Only his business did not prosper, and now he does nothing."

"Where is he?" asked the Prince. "I shall go and find him, and I shall fetch him here…"

The young maiden shook her head slowly.

"You words will be to no avail; no one shall come without florins!"

"And yet I shall try. Your uncle, can he work with wood?"

"Of course he can, he is one of the most skilled craftsmen for weaponry and arms."

"And where would I find him?"

131

"At the tavern, just like everyone else."

"Then I shall go and get him. Prepare a meal for several people," said the Prince, animated. "I will be bringing him to supper."

And with that, he hastened to the capital. He went straight to the tavern. The door was open. Some youths, pale and wretched, were drinking, seated around a filthy rustic table made of rough-hewn wooden boards. Some others, collapsed on the floor, were sleeping heavily, and others still, half-sprawled across the table, were throwing dice or were snoring, their heads resting on their folded arms.

One man, glass in hand, was telling in a husky voice the story of his youth.

The Prince sat across from him. From the similarities in his features, he understood that this was Miserlix's brother.

"Those were the good days, when Prudentius I was still alive and reigning, God rest his soul," the man was saying, sighing deeply. "No man would spend his time drinking in a tavern then; we never even set foot in one."

"And who is forcing you to come here now, old man?" said the Prince.

"Who? Who else but the very wretchedness of this place. How can a man kill time otherwise, except by coming to the tavern? It was different back then. Then we worked. Not like these young lads here!…"

"And why don't you work now, too?"

The man sighed.

"I grew tired of working for no reason and with no sense of purpose," he said with heavy weariness.

The eyes of the Prince were suddenly ablaze.

"Well then, *work now, for a reason and for a purpose*," he said, and his heart was beating thunderously hard in his chest.

"Do you think I would be sitting here if I could find a purpose?!" answered the man.

"Nor would we, old Master Miserlix," said a youth, with the fiery sheen of wine in his eyes. "Offer us some good profit, and you will see with what fervour we will work!"

"For profit or for a purpose?" asked the Prince.

"It is all the same."

"*No*, it is *not* all the same," said the Prince, inflamed with great fire, "for I shall give work to any one of you who wants it. Yet it shall be for a great and sacred purpose, which will yield you no profit."

"You are trying to be funny, countryman!" said the youth, laughing.

"I am not trying to be funny at all. The enemy is right in our midst, marching in our lands!"

The youth rose, leant across the table and looked intently at the Prince.

"What work are you proposing we do?" he asked seriously.

"The work that is the duty of every citizen at a time of national danger."

"You propose to us then to become soldiers and get ourselves killed for the sake of the 'Emperor's New Clothes'?"

"Not for the 'Emperor's New Clothes', but for king and country!"

"Oh, don't bother me with that!" said the youth, his eyes now ablaze. "'Country' is but an empty word, and the King, this king, is but a King Log!"

The insult stung the Prince sharply, burning like a whiplash.

He rose from his chair and, shaking bodily with indignation, he replied:

"The 'country' is your land, and *this king* is your leader!"

A general burst of roaring laughter greeted his words.

"Our provinces over here are secure; the enemy cannot get across the river!" said someone, his voice hoarse from wine-drinking. "And those who happen to live on the other side, well, let them take care of themselves."

"My, what a leader we do have!" cried another. "Hiding behind his windows, that's how he will lead us to war!"

"And without weapons!" added, sniggering, a third.

"*Let the King come out first, and show us how to fight!*" shouted another.

"And if the King comes out, I will myself make weapons for him!" said old Master Miserlix.

Pale as death, arms crossed, the King's son stood up straight in their midst.

"Old Master Miserlix," he said in a thunderous voice, "I have your word! The King is too old by now, and he cannot bear the hardship. Yet his son will come out himself, and you shall make him weapons!"

"Well said," said the old man. "Provided, that is, that the Prince comes out himself."

"*Let the Prince come out,*" said the youth with the fiery eyes, "*and then let us all follow him.*"

The Prince turned to him, and looked at him in the face.

"*Remember* what you have said, *when the time comes,*" he said, his whole being in turmoil; then, turning to the other man: "Old Master Miserlix," he said, "your brother has already started forging the weapons that the Prince will need in order to venture forth with the army. *Will you not help him?*"

The old man was taken aback.

"Do you mean it?" he asked.

"I most certainly do," replied the Prince. "Whenever you wish, come to his house and see for yourself."

He then went out, without looking back.

The old man ran after him, and caught up with him a few paces down the road.

"Won't you explain yourself and your words?" he asked.

"I am the King's son," said the Prince. "I have no florins to pay you with, but I ask you, in the name of our country, to make weapons for me!"

Old Master Miserlix was thunderstruck. He fell down on his knees and remained speechless.

"So, will you come?" asked the Prince.

"Command me, my lord!" muttered the old man. "I am yours!"

The Prince raised him to his feet.

"Have you got your tools with you?" he asked.

"I have!"

"Then come along to your brother's. We must not waste a single hour, and Miserlix awaits us."

Together they went to the blacksmith's house. He had indeed been expecting them, although the hour was late by then. The street urchin alone had eaten and was lying fast asleep in a corner of the back kitchen.

"Tomorrow we shall have more such workers," said Miserlix smiling. "On our way back, we met with one or two other little beggars like him, and the young one told them how he had earned his supper through his work, so I told them to come too. It is to our advantage," Miserlix continued. "While they bring up the ore from the mines, I can work here, so no time is wasted."

They sat at the table. The Prince would not stay, however. He only asked for a slice of bread to eat on the way to the schoolmaster's house, where he still intended to study his letters, before beginning to work with the two master craftsmen.

The schoolmaster's house was far away. He went there running, studied hard, did all his writing, and, still running, he returned to Miserlix's house, where for hours on end they worked the iron, which came red hot out of the smithy furnace.

At midnight, the two brothers abandoned both hammer and lathe.

Miserlix wanted to offer the Prince his own bed. But he did not accept it. He had to go, he said, back to the palace, to learn the news.

Hurriedly he took once more the way to the capital. But he was so worn out that two or three times he had to sit down on the ground to rest. Sleep would overcome him then, and, so as not to yield to it, he would get up and resume his running.

With great effort, he reached the roots of the mountain, and started for the palace. He tried to run, but he was vanquished by exhaustion. He sat on a stone to catch his breath, his eyes closed of their own volition, and he fell into a deep slumber.

XI

Constable or Woodsman?

THIS IS WHERE Little Irene found him, first thing in the morning, on her way to the woods.

She woke him up, and they went down the slope together.

He asked her if she had any more recent news to give him.

"No," she replied. "The enemy has not yet been sighted by the river."

"May God's will be with us!" said the Prince, and his whole heart was in his words. "For us, every hour is to our advantage."

He killed rabbits and game birds with his sling, and divided them into two lots. He also divided the eggs, and took half in his scarf.

"Down below, at Miserlix's house, a great table will be set today, and I must take food there too," he told his sister.

And he recounted to her how he had gone to find Miserlix's brother, who was now also working to make weapons, and how some street urchins were to come and work in the mines, to be paid with the food that he would bring them.

"How lovely!" said Little Irene, deeply moved. "This way you will be feeding quite a number of hungry people, teaching them at the same time to work so that they will no longer be beggars."

"It is exactly what I am striving for," replied the Prince simply. "To teach the people to work once more."

He bade his sister farewell, and ran swiftly back to town.

He went to the schoolmaster's, where he had his lesson, leaving two birds by way of payment. Then he headed for Miserlix's house.

He found everyone hard at work.

On all four of the room's surrounding walls there hung several newly forged weapons.

"This is a splendid start!" said the Prince, delighted. "The enemy has not yet been sighted. Courage! The weapons shall be made."

And after handing the game to Miserlix's daughter, he rolled up his sleeves, and took up the hammer and the tongs.

All of a sudden, however, screams were heard outside.

The Prince abandoned his tools, rushed out, and saw one of the boys from the mines fighting valiantly to save his loaded handcart from two thieves.

The Prince recognized at once the inhospitable man who had chased him and Little Irene away from his doorstep; also the boy who worked for him, and who had stolen Miserlix's watch.

"You scoundrel!" he shouted, and threw himself at him, grabbing him by the throat and laying him flat on the earth.

Miserlix, hearing the screaming, came out too, just as the man's boy was sneaking away to the woods. He chased him, caught him, and brought him back, kicking and screaming.

"Hand me some rope!" cried the Prince.

And with Miserlix's help, he tied their hands behind their backs; they then all went back to the smithy, pushing onwards in front of them the two thieves.

The Prince left the young thief outside, with old Master Miserlix to guard him.

"What you do is shamefully wrong!" cried the thief. "Why have you trussed up our hands as though we were criminals, instead of giving this whippersnapper a good thrashing with the cane for trying to harm honest and peaceful citizens?"

"We shall see about that later," said the Prince. "Now tell me your name."

Suddenly the thief recognized the Prince's face and breathed a sigh of relief. What might he have to fear from a young greenhorn like him?

"Lor' bless us!" he said delightedly. "It's you, isn't it, my lad, you came a day or so ago and knocked at my door? And how is the young girl who was with you then? Would she be your sister, perchance?"

"That too shall be left for later. Now tell me your name."

"Scallywag is my name. But I don't see why you ask me the questions that you should be asking that wastrel who tried to damage our property…"

"I shall ask him too, later. Now tell me why you were trying to take hold of the loaded handcart?"

"Oh, but this is not the way things are, my good lad," said the man, with a foxy smile. "Please allow me to tell you how it all happened. I had been working in the woods, digging and taking out… those things, what d'ya call 'em… them stones. And my boy was there too, helping me. So then, once I had filled my cart, I told my boy to take it home…"

"What did you want the stones for?" asked the Prince.

"To build a chicken coop, bless your heart, because my old one has fallen to ruin. Well then, I heard screams, I went outside, and saw this boy here, who was set upon stealing the stones from my son, and I threw him on the ground to save my own. There, my good lad, that's how the story goes, bless you, my boy. Do now untie my hands, for they have gone numb and blue bound up like this."

"Stay there for now, we have someone else to hear before we can untie you," said the Prince.

And he called now old Master Miserlix, who had been polishing a sword while guarding the thief boy, so as not to waste time.

"Bring him in, old man," he said.

"What is your name and what happened?" he asked the boy.

141

"My name is Mitsos," replied the boy, trembling and secretly making a sign to his father that he had no idea what to say.

The Prince caught sight of the sign, and forced Scallywag to turn his back to the boy.

"Tell them, my boy, weren't you going to…" began the thief.

"You will keep silent, or I shall have you gagged!" shouted the Prince.

"Oh, but my good lad, I only want my boy to tell the truth, so you can believe that he was going—"

Yet, before he could speak another word, Miserlix had muzzled his mouth with a rag.

"Yes," said Mitsos, thinking that he had understood his father's meaning, "I was going to help the boy pull the loaded handcar—"

With a thump of his foot his father stopped him short.

"I mean I was going to take the stones to town to sell them to the master blacksm—"

Another thump of the foot, and the boy completely lost his wits, bursting into tears.

"Enough!" said the Prince.

And he called in the boy from the mine:

"Tell us what happened, Thanos?"

"I was returning from the mineshafts, with the ore stones," said Thanos, "and this one came out of the woods and grabbed hold of the handcart. I shouted to him that this was another man's property, when the older

142

one came too, threw me to the ground, and he would have taken the handcart from me if you had not arrived at the scene."

"Did you hear that, Master Scallywag?" said the Prince. "You did not know of course that the handcart belonged to us, and that this boy works in our workshop, or else you would have conjured up some other story to tell us. And you, Mitsos," he continued, turning to the thief boy, "now that you have had the good fortune to cross paths with Master Miserlix again, won't you return to him the watch that you have been keeping for some days now in your breast pocket?"

Everyone was confounded by the Prince's words. Scallywag alone understood; his knees then failed him, and he collapsed on a chair.

The Prince took the watch and its chain from the thief's pocket, and returned them to Miserlix.

"My watch!" exclaimed the blacksmith with delight. "How did it come to be in this boy's pocket?"

In a few words, the Prince recounted all that he had heard and seen from behind the loose pile of rubble at the back of the thief's house.

"And now," he said, "forwards! *March!*"

He led them, arms tied behind their backs, to prison, and found the jailor chatting at the door with a young man.

With displeasure the Prince recognized the drunken youth with the wine-glazed eyes, who had uttered such insults against the King in the tavern.

He too recognized him, and asked sarcastically: "Hey there, countryman! So then, has the King's son come out yet?"

The Prince did not answer. He asked for the keys and the jailor handed them to him, bowing all the way to the ground.

He crossed the square to the other side where the prison cells stood, opened the door, and locked the thieves in.

The youth and the jailor stared at him as he went.

"Tell me one thing, why did you bow so deeply when you handed him the keys?" asked the youth. "Who is he?"

"I don't know," replied the jailor. "Only he made Master Faintheart take Miserlix out of prison, when it had been Faintheart himself who had sentenced him."

"My, you don't say!" said the youth.

And he went on contemptuously:

"He must be some palace lackey or other... Same as the rest of them..."

"Not at all!" said the jailor. "It was a palace man who asked for Miserlix's jail sentence. Master Faintheart who sentenced an innocent man had sold himself heart and soul to the palace men. He, though!... You should have seen him! He was driving Master Faintheart with a whip, and he forced him to take the innocent man out of prison."

"With a what, did you say?"

"With a whip!" repeated the jailor.

The Prince locked the prison door, brought back the keys and turned to go.

"Who can he be?" muttered the youth.

And from a distance, he followed him.

Going past the house of Illstar the master builder, the Prince decided to go up and ask him whether he had set himself down to work yet.

"The master builder is not upstairs," shouted the cobbler, who had his workshop around the corner. "He is down by the river."

"This is good!" the Prince thought joyfully to himself. "So, he has already started work then!"

He turned towards the river, but as he was passing the woods he heard voices.

He entered the woods, and amongst the trees he saw some youths who were struggling to pull an enormous log, all trussed up with ropes. But the log was heavy, and they could not make it yield an inch.

"Where do you wish to take this?" asked the Prince.

"To the river, where the foreman wants it," they replied.

"It is impossible to drag it like this. It is too big."

"And what are we to do? The foreman needs it. We shall be spitting blood by the end of it, but drag it we shall."

"You will break your ropes, and still you shall have achieved nothing. We must find some other way. You need wheels…"

The lumbermen laughed.

"And that is just what we do not have!" they said.

The Prince took a few moments to think.

"Hand me your axe," he said.

145

And removing his jerkin, the Prince fashioned three rollers. These they placed under the log. All three of them harnessed themselves with the ropes, and together they pulled. The log rolled forward, as though on wheels.

"And when the log rolls forward, beyond the last roller, you must take that one and put it again in front of the log," the Prince told them. "In this fashion, you will be able to roll it along all the way to the river."

The two young men thanked him, overjoyed.

"You cannot know how much easier you have made our task," they said, relieved, "and how happy the foreman will be now that the transport will move faster."

"Who is your foreman?" asked the Prince.

"Illstar the master builder."

"And how is it that you work for him? I thought he no longer had apprentices."

"And he didn't. He had been working alone since his affairs went bad," replied one of the young men. "He had even closed his workshop down. Only he must have received some really fine commission, for he sold his house and everything he had, and hired us all, every wood craftsman in town, with good wages, so that we might work night and day."

"Here's to him, here's to a good countryman!" cried the Prince with fervour.

And he ran down to the river.

As he was hastening ahead, he stumbled on a man who stood there unnoticed.

"Constable or woodsman?" the man asked.

The Prince turned around and recognized the youth from the tavern.

"Both," he replied.

"And something else perhaps?" asked the young man.

The Prince looked him straight in the eye.

"Yes," he said. "And something else besides."

And with that he ran away.

At a turning in the road, he met with some villagers, fleeing in terror towards the town.

"Where are you running?" he cried out to them.

The villagers, however, did not reply. They hurried on, without stopping.

A few yards farther down the road, he saw another five or six men, who were running away as well.

The Prince approached them.

"Where to, countrymen?" he asked.

"To the capital," they replied. "Do not go that way, the enemy will arrive at any time!"

"Arrive where?"

They did not reply. Scared and dazed, they left, scurrying as fast as they could.

The Prince ran after them, caught up with them.

"Why are you going away?!" he asked angrily. "What are you afraid of that you run away like bolting rabbits?"

"The enemy has reached the shore across the river," answered one of the men.

"And so what?! There is still the river. How will they cross it? Come back to your senses, countrymen; do not lose your good judgement, in God's name! Are you frail little women, to scare so easily?" cried the Prince, all flared up. "To arms, lads! We shall stop them!"

The villagers came to a halt for a moment.

"But we have no weapons!" they said.

"Get hold of anything sharp that you may have: a knife, a sickle, an axe or a mattock, and follow me!"

"Who will lead us?" asked one of the men, jittery with fear.

"I shall!" said the Prince with great force. "Come back. For God's sake, do not go away!"

"Pah!" said another. "And why should we fight? If the river stops the enemy, then we who are on this side have nothing to worry about. If, however, the river cannot halt them, then neither could we. Why should we get killed for no reason? We will do no more nor less than the King and the Prince are doing themselves."

"The King shall stay! The Prince shall lead you! No one is leaving; stay, stay too!"

One of the villagers laughed scornfully.

"Why don't you go and find out what is going on in the palace?" he said. "The King is getting ready to steal away, and the Prince has already fled!"

"The Prince has not fled! He is in your midst!" shouted the Prince. "Look at me, countrymen! I am the King's son, and I shall lead you!"

"Go on with you, go tell your tall tales somewhere else!" said the villagers. "They saw the Prince crossing the river last night; he ran away abroad the moment he felt that things were getting tight! And so shall we!"

The Prince pressed his hands hard on his forehead.

What was he to do? How could he keep them from running away?

He thought of the King, who was sure to be going mad in the palace, all alone. He remembered the words that had come out of the peasant's mouth: "The King is getting ready to steal away…"

Terror seized him; he turned back and, running like mad, he scaled the mountainside.

XII

Panic

T HE PEOPLE were coming down from the villages in great hordes; they ran to the capital without rhyme or reason, frenzied by fear. The Prince strove to stop them, but panic had rendered them deaf and blind.

"We have no King! We have no country!" they would say.

And nothing could restrain them.

The Prince reached the palace at long last.

The doors had all been thrown wide open. The King's family had gathered in the dining hall, resembling a gaggle of frightened geese. All the women were shrieking together; the King, with his mantle draped over his arm, was giving imperious orders to imaginary servants to shut the windows, tidy up the disorder and such like. Little Irene was sitting huddled in a corner, crying with heavy sobs. Dragging a great big chest behind him, Polycarpus would turn around now and then to look at her, and he would despair at not being able to console her.

"What *is* all this? *What* is all this *dreadfulness* that goes on in here?" said the Prince in a thundering voice.

Everyone turned around. The women ceased their shrieking, Little Irene ran and hung herself from his neck, the King let out a sigh of relief, and Polycarpus let go of the chest.

"What *is* the matter? *Why* all this confusion?" the Prince asked again.

And his warm voice rose high above the chaos, reassuring every frightened heart.

"Oh, my son! Wherefore did you go!" said the King plaintively. "Is this a time to go wandering about?"

"Abandoning us to our own devices, leaving us helpless to face our fate, to go all on our own to foreign lands!" added the Queen.

"What?" cried the Prince. "Who talks of going away?"

"You *had* abandoned us, my son," pleaded the King, trying to excuse himself, "and we did not know what to do and where to go…"

"*Everyone* is leaving; we shall leave as well," added the Queen.

"*No one* is to leave!" said the Prince with determination.

"You would not presume to try to stop us, I hope!" screeched Spitefulnia.

"*No one* is going anywhere!" repeated the Prince, even more loudly. "You, the women, go to your rooms. And you, father, come downstairs with me. It is absolutely vital that you show yourself in public immediately."

"Where do you want us to go?" asked the King rather fearfully.

"To the capital, so that the panic-stricken people will all see us and follow us."

"But follow us where?"

Before the Prince had time to answer, however, the Lord Chamberlain tumbled and rolled into the room.

His hanging cheeks were flashing red and fiery, his eyes bulging violently out of his skull.

"My lord! My lord! The enemy is burning the land across the river, they have set fire to the woods, the entire plain is being ravaged by the flames as we speak! The people, gathered by the riverside and in the town square, are in the throes of frenzy, howling insults against you for not being there to lead them, to help their brothers who are in dire peril on the opposite riverbank. My lord, the enemy advances! Soon they will have reached the river!…"

The King turned to his son in despair.

"So much the better!" said the Prince with clenched teeth.

"My child! What are you saying! We are losing half our kingdom!" exclaimed the King.

"*So much the better!*" repeated the Prince more loudly. "Now is the time to hold the wolf by the ears! Now we know the truth, we feel the burn of the whiplash."

"But they are insulting the throne! The State is as good as lost! There is an uprising in the capital…" grunted the Lord Chamberlain. "They no longer wish to have a monarchy…"

"And who gives a brass farthing about the throne or about the monarchy?!" cried the Prince. "The nation is alive, it is finally awake, and bodily it shall rise, quash the enemies who are trampling the nation's land! Father, come, *now*!"

And dragging the King by the arm, he trundled hurriedly down the mountain.

"You, run ahead of us!" he cried to Polycarpus, who was following him. "Go to Miserlix's workshop, take the weapons that are ready, and bring them all immediately down to the river. That is where I shall assemble everyone."

Mayhem reigned everywhere. The townsmen were hurling their belongings out of windows, loading them onto carts or on the backs of mules, striving to escape to the safety of the mountains, whereas the villagers were escaping in turn to the capital, there seeking safety.

Everyone had lost their minds; no one knew what they were doing.

"Peace, lads, we have nothing to fear," the Prince would tell them as he passed them by.

And to the women he would say:

"Go to your houses, and have no fear!"

When he arrived at the square with the King, they saw gathered in front of the barracks a great throng of people, shouting and clamouring for an army. At one of the windows, his hair bristling, eyes bulging, the garrison commander, still wrapped in his blanket, kept screaming back that he had no army, and that they should go and ask for one from the King.

"We have no King. The King has left and has abandoned us. Down with the King! Down with the monarchy!" the throng shouted.

"Oh, *do* let us go away!" pleaded the King, leaning heavily on his son's arm. Hear how they abuse us!"

"No!" said the Prince with resolve. "Either we shall die here, or here shall we prevail upon them!"

Making his way through the crowd, he managed to get ahead; he then climbed to the top of the steps reaching the entryway of the garrison tower.

"Countrymen, what is it you seek?" he cried loudly, and his voice was heard clearly, rising strong above the noise, from one corner of the square to the other. "What are you lingering here for, when the enemy is ravaging our land? *Have courage in your hearts, lads, and let us all march forward! Follow me!* Together we shall drive the enemy away!"

"We have no army! We don't even have weapons!" cried some in the crowd.

"The army is you! Why do you look for it elsewhere, since you are all gathered here? The tools with which you till your fields will be your weapons and your armaments! In the hands of the valiant, any piece of iron becomes a mighty weapon!"

"We have no leader! The King has fled abroad!"

"Your King is here, among you, ready to lead you into battle!" cried the Prince, pointing to his aged father, who, before the enraged populace, had found once more his ancestral dignity and pride, and was gazing at the angered crowd with arms crossed, his head held high.

"Where is the King? Show us the King!" shouted some.

"Our King has not left? The King is here?" cried out some others. "*Then long live the King!*"

"*If* the King is here, *ask him first for arms!*" called out an angry voice.

"Yes, arms! Give us arms!" repeated more voices.

And the crowd, always ready to follow the last speaker, roared angrily:

"*Give us arms! Down with the King! Oust the King and away with him!*"

Some, even more brazenly audacious, clambered up the steps brandishing their fists menacingly.

"Give us arms! Down with the King! Oust the King and away with him!" they screamed.

The Prince threw himself in front of his father and with a push sent rolling down a man who was raising his arm to strike at the King.

"When real men have no arms," he shouted with hot indignation, they go and get them from the enemy; they do not strike out at old men!"

"Here's to you, my fine lad! Well answered!" sounded a voice.

And the human throng, once again ready to follow the last speaker who had prevailed over it, cried out:

"Here's to you, fine lad! You lead and we shall follow you! Long live our Prince! Long live the King!"

Wasting no time, the Prince commanded:

"Forwards, then! To the river! There we shall muster our forces, so we may cross to the other side and drive the enemy away! Come on, men! Follow me!"

Exhausted and choking with emotion, the King went up to the garrison commander's office to rest—while the Prince headed for the river, with the animated crowd shouting and following hard upon his heels.

XIII

Polydorus and Onearm

T HROUGHOUT THAT DAY *Fright* and *Turmoil* had
gone back and forth many times between the two
riverbanks, in order to ferry across the villagers from the
great plain who were fleeing before the enemy.

When he had brought over the last passenger, instead
of marooning his feluccas on solid land and lying in his
"chambers" as he was wont to do, the one-armed man
set off northwards up the river, pushing his boats with
the punt pole.

Illstar the master builder, who was working by the water's
edge, saw him and called out to him:

"Where to, countryman?"

"Secret mission of the State," replied the one-armed man.
Then he added:

"I am assuming that it is for peacetime that you toil so,
master builder?"

"How would you know what I am doing?" asked the
master builder.

"Do you think I am blind? You think I can't see that you are building huge and mighty ships?"

"And by your reckoning, then, these are for peacetime?"

"Of course they must be: you will never finish them afore nightfall; and before the sun has set, our guests will be all lined up across the river."

The master builder dropped what he was doing and went nearer to the water.

"You know that what you have just said is dead right?" he said earnestly.

"You flatter me, countryman," replied the one-armed man, going up to the prow and trailing his punt pole behind him.

The master builder was pensive.

"So what do you suggest I do?" he said all of a sudden.

"Build a bridge," replied the one-armed man.

"A bridge? And do you imagine, then, that a bridge can be built in three hours?"

The one-armed man took his cable and showed it to him.

"With this it can be," he said.

And pointing at the felled logs piled high on the river-bank, ready to be sawn:

"And with these," he added.

And he started again on his way, propelling his feluccas northwards up the river and muttering gloomily:

> *Robbers have taken to the mountains,*
> *Horses will they be a-stealing…*

158

For some time, the master builder remained immobile, following the feluccas with pensive eyes. Then suddenly he slapped his forehead:

"But of course! He is right, he is, that one!" he murmured.

And he gave out instantly new instructions to his assistants:

"Abandon all work on the ships everyone, at once! And come here. I have a pressing task to give you."

The one-armed man, however, continued pacing from stern to prow, thrusting his punt pole into the water, and humming:

> *Yet horses they could find none,*
> *Young lambs they snatched in their stead…*

As he moved northwards, however, the water current became ever stronger, and in the end it was so powerful that he could no longer steer with his punt pole.

He headed for the riverbank on his right, and when he had approached it sufficiently with his feluccas, he leapt to the shore.

He uncoiled the rope, tied it around his waist, and slowly, but at a steady pace, he walked up along the riverbank, tugging his home behind him.

The water was running southward with great momentum, yet the one-armed man did not stop. Rivers of sweat trickled down his forehead, his mouth was parched, his tongue was panting, the veins and arteries on his neck were swollen to bursting point from the great endeavour. His steady step, however, never faltered.

He reached Fool's Eddy, tied the rope around a tree, and lay down on the grass to regain his breath.

Suddenly he heard the mad galloping of a horse. The one-armed man rose, yet before he could make out what was happening, the horse and its rider had charged out from the woods and collapsed in front of him.

In the flicker of a second, the rider untangled himself from the stirrups, and got up from the ground.

The one-armed man with a leap ran then to the tree, and cut the rope.

"*Quick!*" he cried. "*Jump inside.*"

He leapt into the boat with Polydorus, and pulled in the remaining length of rope.

The current carried them off, and the feluccas found themselves instantly midstream, moving southwards at great speed.

At that very moment, a great cloud of arrows flew out of the woods, falling in a shower around them, splattering the two men with spray as they struck the water.

And the riverbank swarmed up with soldiers.

The one-armed man saluted them with a low bow.

"You may shoot all you want, now!" he cried out.

Indeed, the river, very rapid and somewhat wider at that point, was taking them farther and farther away from the enemy's side.

The one-armed man had gathered up his rope and was tidying it up calmly.

"Did you accomplish your mission?" he asked.

"Yes!" replied Polydorus.

"Yet you rode your horse to its death."

"It was one of their own. I took it from them. Mine died earlier on the way. But tell me, how did you know I would get here so fast and manage to be at our meeting point on time?"

"You were in a hurry. I knew that if you could find a horse, you would take it. I reckoned that you would be galloping whip and spur."

"You reckoned well. Had you not been there, as if by some miracle, I might never have lived to see again the bright eyes of the Prince, and for their sake I would sacrifice my very life!"

The bargeman, after coiling the rope neatly on the prow, came and sat by the equerry's side.

"Do not rejoice quite so soon," he said quietly, "for you have not seen them yet, those eyes you speak of."

Polydorus shuddered.

"What do you mean?" he asked.

The one-armed man nodded towards the mainland with his head.

"Our guests are following us," he said.

"Yes, I can see them, but they are far away. The river is broad, and their arrows cannot reach us."

"They will, farther south."

"The river narrows there?"

"Yes."

The equerry paused for some time to gather his thoughts.

"Is there nothing to be done?" he asked.

"Yes, there is. I shall take my punt pole when the time comes. Now it's of no use. The river carries us more swiftly."

"Whatever it should take, I must get through," said the equerry.

And he asked:

"You know these parts well?"

"Yes."

"And do you think we can get through the strait?"

"No, I don't."

"Onearm," said the equerry, "*one of us must get through*."

And pointing to the large leather money belt around his waist, he added:

"This must be delivered into the hands of the Prince."

The one-armed man smiled.

"Well, then, put it rather in my bedroom," he said. "My house will always get through. You or I, however, might not come out of this alive."

"But if the risk is so great, why don't we get ashore now?" asked Polydorus.

"You say you are in a hurry to get to where you are going."

"Yes! But we could reach the capital on foot."

"There is no path."

"We can cross the mountain."

"Only of you had wings could you get through that way. The crevasses are impenetrable, and the mountain snow eternal," replied the one-armed man.

"And is there no other way?"

"A speedy way, you mean? No, there is none."

For some time the river carried them on, each sunk in his own silence.

They gazed without speaking at the waters, which tapered sharply to a narrow bottleneck between the riverbanks.

All of a sudden, the one-armed man rose to his feet; he seized his punt pole and he thrust it with great force into the riverbed. *Fright* and *Turmoil* swivelled around abruptly and came out of the midstream, heading towards the left bank.

"What is the matter?" asked Polydorus.

The one-armed man, however, had no time to reply, for five or six arrows dug themselves viciously into the sides of the feluccas; at the same time, several riders in full armour appeared through the trees on their right.

"The fun is about to begin," said the one-armed man.

The current was strong at the straits, and the bargeman could only steer his boats with extreme effort. He knew he could not get too close to the left bank: at the roots of the mountain, black rocks, which jutted out now and then from beneath the waters, posed a nasty hazard for the old rotting timbers of *Fright* and *Turmoil*.

"Are we still far away?" asked the equerry.

"No," replied the one-armed man. "If we can make it past the strait, we shall be safe."

And bending down swiftly, he dodged an arrow, which flew past him only to bury itself into Polydorus's shoulder.

Pulling out his punt pole, the one-armed man hurried to the equerry's side.

"You have been wounded!" he cried out.

"It is nothing, barely a scratch," replied the equerry. "But for God's sake, plunge in your punt pole, push, the current is carrying us back midstream once more."

The one-armed man ran to the prow and thrust his punt pole into the riverbed.

Yet suddenly his legs buckled under him; he advanced but a single step, lunged bodily forward, and fell into the water.

"*Onearm!*" cried Polydorus frantically.

"Preseeeent…" came the drowning voice of the one-armed man.

For one instant longer his bloodied face lingered on the watery surface. He stretched out his hand for help—perhaps for a final farewell—and then the river covered him with its silver shroud.

The arrows came whistling like a hailstorm all around the feluccas, which were being carried midstream yet again.

Polydorus had seized the punt pole and with great force he was thrusting it into the riverbed.

At that same instant, an arrow pierced his brow and threw him down on his knees. He hurriedly wiped away the blood that was blinding him, and tried to stand up. Yet another arrow dug itself into his chest; the punt pole slipped through his hands, and was carried away by the river.

Seeing that the youth had been wounded, the riders burst into wild yawps of triumph and, using him as a target, competed with one another to see who could drive more arrows into his fallen body.

One of these arrows struck him in the neck; another slashed the strap of his money belt, and some florins spilt out.

He raised himself up with great effort, and rebuckled the strap. But another arrow pierced his side, and he collapsed onto the bottom of the boat.

"Mother, sweet, loving mother…" he muttered.

It seemed to him that the sun had been extinguished, and that blackest night had spread everywhere.

The current was carrying away *Fright* and *Turmoil*, propelling them out of the strait towards the broad river below, where they continued to travel slowly on its becalmed waters.

From under the riverside trees, where he was working with feverish zeal, the master builder made out from afar the twin boats. He thought it strange that he could not see the one-armed man pushing his punt pole, or lying on the prow as he was wont to do, so he cried out to him:

"Ahoy there, countryman! Where are you hiding?"

No one replied. And the boats were coming nearer, ever faster. He thought he could make out a body lying down, but it did not look like the bargeman's.

"Countryman! Ahoy there, Onearm!" he cried out again. But no reply was heard.

The master builder wasted no time. With the help of his assistants, he threw onto the water the pontoon he was building, and jumped aboard.

"Easy with the ropes there, lads, till I can get midway across the river," he cried.

From the opposite bank, where the enemy was now encamped, some of the soldiers shot arrows at him and shouted insults.

"Long live the Royal Navy of Witless I!" one of them jeered.

And at that, all the others broke into rude and rowdy laughter.

Unperturbed, the master builder allowed the feluccas to get close enough, till they finally collided with the pontoon and their movement was arrested for a moment. Instantly, he grabbed then the rope that was coiled on the prow, and motioned to his men to pull him back to the shore.

XIV

The Battle

T HE PRINCE had come to the river. He concealed his men in the woods, and instructed them not to come out from the trees, so that the enemy would not see them.

His plan was to cross to the opposite bank during the night, assail the sleeping camp with his men, and, taking advantage of the resulting mayhem and the fright that would seize the enemy, drive them far away. There he would strive to hold them, by any means available to him, until he had formed an army and a navy, and then, by fighting hard, force them to the other side of the border.

In order to succeed in his purpose, however, he had to find a way to ferry his soldiers across.

He was going therefore at once to seek Illstar, and propose his plan to him.

From the distance, he saw under the trees many men gathered together, and the master builder bending over a human body that lay on the ground.

"What is the matter?" he asked, drawing near.

The master builder recognized his voice, and turned around. His face was ashen and unsmiling.

"You are the one he asked for, my lord," he said without rising.

"Who did?" asked the Prince.

And pushing the workmen aside, he bent and saw the bloodied face, where the arrow remained still buried deep in the furrows of his brow.

"Polydorus!" cried the Prince, and fell on his knees by his side.

He lifted up the equerry's head, held it against his chest, and wiped the blood that dripped from the wet hair.

"Fetch some water, quick!" he ordered.

"It won't do any good, my lord," said the master builder, "the gallant youth is dead…"

"That cannot be! He must live! *He must!*" cried the Prince. "Polydorus… can you hear me! Speak to me…"

He received no reply. The pursed lips remained mute, turned into the marble of eternal silence.

With nervous fingers he pushed away the leather money belt in order to feel whether the heart was beating. The strap came undone, and golden florins spilt out on the dusty earth.

The Prince stood up then, and turned to his men.

"Soldiers!" he cried, and his voice was quivering with the turmoil in his soul. "This noble youth gave up his life willingly for the sake of his country; he has shown you the way to glory. From each of you tonight I expect the same sacrifice, whether it may be to death that I lead you, or to victory! Countrymen! Hail the first fallen hero!"

Everyone around him knelt down in silence.

They buried the valiant youth there where his life's breath had flown away from him. In the grave where the Prince had laid him, his arms crossed upon his chest, Polydorus now slept his final sleep. A bitter smile had frozen on his lips. The light of his eyes had been snuffed out without their meeting the bright gaze of his lord, who had awakened in his soul so much beauty and such strength, and had transformed him from a mere average man into a hero.

With heavy hearts they all went back to their tasks, for time was passing, and the enemy had drawn very close.

"Master builder," said the Prince, "I have a plan for tonight. But in order for it to succeed, I need your help."

"Command me, my lord," replied the master builder. "Whatever it is you wish, I shall do it."

"I know you sold everything you had, your house even, so you might pay the workers and build me a navy…"

"I only did my duty," said the master builder simply.

The Prince stretched his hand out to him.

"I thank you in the name of our country," he said, deeply affected in his heart. "But now, I must ask you to abandon your ships. I have need of something much more urgent."

"I have abandoned them already, my lord. Tell me what it is you want."

"With the army that I have at my disposal, I cannot possibly tackle a regular trained army. I have decided therefore to take the enemy by surprise, strike against their camp tonight with my soldiers, and drive them away. But we will have to cross the river."

"And you have no ships, is that what you mean to say, my lord?"

"I thought that you might be able to build me a makeshift bridge—" began the Prince.

The master builder, however, interrupted him.

"I have it all but ready," he said.

The Prince was much astonished.

"Who told you to make it?" he asked.

"The one-armed man," replied the master builder.

And he recounted to the Prince the words he had exchanged with the bargeman.

"So I have built you many pontoons," he continued. "At your command, we shall quietly and silently tie one pontoon to the next, and the entire army will cross to the other side."

"Where is the bargeman?" asked the Prince excitedly. "I must speak to him at once!"

"I don't know," answered the master builder. "Since the time when he went up the river, I have not seen him at all. The wounded youth was found in his feluccas, yet the bargeman was not with him."

"He did not tell you where he was going when you asked him?"

"No. He only said: 'Secret mission of the State!' I did not understand what he meant."

"And Polydorus said nothing to you?"

"He did not have the time," replied the master builder. "He was unconscious when I laid him on the ground, drenched in blood. I tried to bring him round, but he never opened his eyes again. He murmured your name once or twice, and then he died."

"When the one-armed man comes back tonight, I want to see him," said the Prince. The one-armed man, however, never returned.

The night was well advanced. Everything was ready.

The Prince had organized his soldiers in units, after having distributed to them the arms as well as all the sickles, scythes, hoes and every other tool brought to him by the villagers.

In a low voice he was giving out his final orders, while by the river the master builder and his apprentices were tying together the pontoons one beside the other, and securing them to the riverbank.

The Prince gave the signal, and stepped onto the bridge, crossing first to the other side.

The enemy camp was sleeping most serenely.

The King the Royal Uncle had reached the river without ever meeting a single soldier. Before him, the country dwellers ran away in terrified throngs, abandoning their villages, which the enemy burned down after having despoiled the houses of all that they could carry.

He had no reason to worry, the King the Royal Uncle, nor did his soldiers. And, weary from the day's long march, they slept heavily, without even thinking of posting a watch.

The Prince realized immediately the advantage such negligence had given him.

Noiselessly, muffling the sound of their steps, the Fatalists surrounded the camp, and, holding their breath, waited for the signal.

A fire signal flashed all of a sudden near the riverbank.

There, the Prince, before any other man, unsheathed his sword and hurled himself upon the enemy, and from every side the soldiers followed him, rending the air with mighty yowls.

Their foes woke up in terror from the clamour.

At first they could not make out what was happening, and the Prince's soldiers had time to slay a good number of them before they were able to think about reassembling themselves.

It wasn't long before they realized, however, that some unknown enemy had assailed them; then they ran for their arms.

Only it was not an easy task to find them in the solid darkness of the moonless night. In the meantime, the soldiers of the Prince were cutting down their enemies with their long scythes; like stalks of wheat, they fell upon the ground.

Panic seized the enemy and they sought to escape towards the plains, hoping to save their lives. But the Prince was on the lookout for them, and with a few chosen soldiers he fell upon them and killed so many that the blood flowed like a river on the ground.

"Onwards! *Onwards!*" cried the Prince. "*Onwards, men!* Let us capture their king."

And sword in hand, he ran to the tent of the King the Royal Uncle.

The King, however, was a daring man. He would not give himself up so easily. He woke up at the first sound of screaming, grabbed hold of his armour and weapons at once, and tried to recall his soldiers to order.

Master Faintheart was shaking so terribly that he could not even stand up on his feet; helpless, he sat down heavily on the ground.

"Pick up your sword, you coward!" his ally yelled at him. "Pick up your weapons and follow me! You are the one who got me into this, and lured me into waging this war. Come out now and fight at my side."

Master Faintheart, however, could no longer move a muscle; the King the Royal Uncle kicked him aside with disgust and went out of his tent.

Seeing his men run away, his anger turned into frenzy and he began to hit them with the pole of his lance. He managed to muster a few together, and with these he strove to offer some resistance, shouting:

"You spineless cowards! Where are you running away to? Are you lambs with a wolf at your heels? Come back! Come stand by your king, and see if he knows how to fight for your sake!"

With his cries, he stopped a few more.

"Let us to the river, now! If they could cross the waters, so can we, and get ourselves to the other side. And when they see us arriving at their homes, they will scatter away like frightened sparrows! Come, lads! To the river!"

The Prince saw him though. He realized immediately what total devastation would ensue should the enemy cross to the left bank where there wasn't a soldier of theirs left.

With his few select men, he rushed to the bridge, arriving at the very moment when the small unit of men guarding it was almost at the end of its tether, and just as the first enemy soldiers were leaping onto the pontoons.

"Break up the bridge! Master builder, cut the ropes!" he bellowed. "And if any of our own men try to escape, then let them be drowned by the river!"

From the opposite bank, the master builder heard him; he leapt onto the bridge and with two hacks of his axe he split it in two.

The pontoon bridge was divided into two halves.

The enemy forces, seeing the way severed, tried to turn back. But all of a sudden, from amidst the companions of the Prince, there leapt out a youth, who ran to the river, and at the risk of his life, defying the lances of the enemy, slashed through the ropes which still secured the pontoons to the mainland; half the bridge was thus swept away by the current, together with all the enemy soldiers who had had time to leap on to it.

The youth then disappeared, was lost once more amidst the soldiers.

The Prince fought as fiercely as a lion, and his example gave heart even to the most timorous of men.

The King the Royal Uncle saw him, and recognized him in the blaze of the fire that still burned on the shore.

"Lads! My steed, my fighting arms, *my daughter too* shall I give to the man who brings me that youth, alive or dead."

His most select officers and men pounced to seize him.

Yet the Prince's sword was reaping heads, clearing a circle around him. A knife blow had slashed his forehead, yet the Prince continued to hack away, and the enemy, dazzled by his boldness, had begun to shirk away and retreat—when, all of a sudden, his sword blade broke in his hands.

With wild howls they sprang upon him then. One man thrust his spear with such force into his shoulder that the Prince fell down on his knees.

They would certainly have slaughtered him. But in a flash the same youth who had slashed the rope of the bridge leapt out from the crowd again, and with his own body he shielded the Prince.

"Leave, my lord!" he shouted.

In an instant, ten swords pierced him through and through. And he collapsed unconscious, drenched in his own blood.

That instant had been sufficient. Seeing their Prince fallen on the ground, the Fatalists transformed into fierce

175

beasts, and with renewed resolve assailed their enemies, pushed them back, quashed them, forced them into mad retreat.

The enemy King himself had barely enough time to escape, and, seeing the battle lost, he leapt onto his horse and turned tail towards the plains, followed by the pitiful remnants of his army.

The Prince, kneeling on the ground, overmastering his wounds, was striving to bring around the youth who had saved him by sacrificing his own life.

"Hand me a light!" he commanded.

And they fetched him immediately a lighted torch.

Under the flame of the torch, he recognized the young man from the tavern.

"He, *of all men*, here!…" he muttered.

He took a water bottle from a fallen enemy, and poured some drops between the wounded man's parted lips.

The youth opened his eyes, saw the Prince leaning over him, and smiled.

"Constable, woodsman… *and prince*…" he said with great effort. "You see… I did remember my own words when the time came… The Prince came out, and we all followed him…"

He closed his eyes, and his head dropped slowly to the side.

"Please forget the other words I said," he murmured with a voice that was fading, "and forgive me."

The Prince bent down and embraced him.

"You saved my life today," he said, deeply troubled and moved in his heart, "and by your courage, when you cut away the bridge you destroyed many enemies. What forgiveness would you be asking for?"

Yet the youth gave no reply, nor did he ever stir again. In the Prince's arms, death had taken him.

XV

Justice

MISERLIX HAD BEEN FIGHTING at the other end of the enemy camp, and had been busy for some time chasing away a good few of the enemy; not seeing the Prince as he came back, he asked where he was.

No one knew.

Deeply alarmed, he sought him here and there; as he was doing so, some soldiers near the tent of the King the Royal Uncle cried out to him.

"Come here, Master Miserlix, we have something we want to show you," they said.

And they all burst out laughing.

Between them they were holding up a man from under his arms. His head was sunk on his chest, his hair was dishevelled, his plush, wine-red velvet tabard all white from the dust. And as soon as the soldiers loosened their support, he slid to the ground.

"What is the matter with this poor soul?" asked Miserlix. "Is he wounded or ill?"

The soldiers again burst out laughing.

"Neither the one nor the other," they replied. "It's just that he is shaking all over from fear."

Miserlix approached, with the intention of sending the soldiers away and of setting the man free. When he had a closer look at him, however, he stopped short.

"The Judge!" he cried out.

As soon as Master Faintheart heard Miserlix's voice, his knees buckled entirely under him, and, slipping through the soldiers' hands, he collapsed spread-eagled onto the dusty ground.

"Where was he?" asked Miserlix. "How come he did not escape with the others?"

"Do not ask how we found him!" said one of the soldiers. "We entered the tent of the King to gather up his things and take them to the Prince, when we saw there a seat covered with a rug. A friend of mine sat on it to rest, and suddenly the seat crumbled down and my friend fell on his back. We were frightened that perhaps we had broken something valuable and precious, and so we lifted up the rug hastily. And what did we see then? His lordship, half-dead with fright!"

Miserlix gazed at him with disgust.

"Gather him up and bring him to the Prince," he ordered. "His Highness will himself decide his fate."

And again he went looking for the Prince.

He found him sitting by a tree trunk, his head bandaged with a scarf. A soldier, who happened to be a doctor, was washing and dressing the wound on his shoulder.

At his feet lay the bloodied body of the youth, and the Prince pointed him out to Miserlix.

"He let himself be killed to save me," he said hoarsely.

"He did what anyone amongst us would have done," replied Miserlix.

Sweet daybreak was approaching fast.

The men, tired and hungry, were garnering from the enemy tents anything they could find to eat, and were preparing to lie down and sleep.

At that moment, some soldiers arrived, dragging Master Faintheart behind them.

"Not now," Miserlix said to them. "His Highness is exhausted."

The Prince heard him, however, and wanted to know what the matter was.

When he saw and recognized the Judge, he ordered that he be brought before him.

"Master Faintheart, what explanation can you give for your own presence here?" he asked him.

The unperturbed manner of the Prince soothed Master Faintheart's fears, and immediately he grew bold.

"Oh, my lord!" he moaned. "If *only* you knew what *miseries* I have been through since I last saw you. I had to go away, poor man that I am, to save myself from Cunningson, who would *most surely* have killed me if he ever found out what I told you! Only, from one single fright I found myself in a *thrice-worse predicament*! I crossed to the neighbouring kingdom, and before I knew what had happened, they had seized me and dragged me, against my will, to the King your Royal Uncle."

He paused for a moment, and cast a foxy glance around him, to make sure everyone believed him.

"Well, then?" asked the Prince quietly.

"Well then, the King your Royal Uncle told me that he intended to conquer the kingdom of the King your father, and offered me great honours and riches if I were to guide him here. *But of course I would not hear of such a thing!*"

And again he looked around him, although with less self-assurance this time. Everyone's profound silence seemed unpleasant to him.

"And so?" the Prince said.

"I replied to him that I would rather die a thousand times than accept such an offer," Master Faintheart went on. "And the King your Royal Uncle became furious, and he tied me to a horse, and brought me hither shackled in chains. God has shown me his mercy by granting you victory, and you have released me from the hands of that cruel monarch!"

He crossed himself, wiped his eyes, and repeated in a quavering voice:

"God has shown me his mercy!"

The Prince then took out of his pocket a crumpled and bloodstained piece of paper, unfolded it, and laid it in front of the Judge.

"Do you recognize this?" he asked.

As Master Faintheart took a look and recognized the

letter that he had written to Cunningson, he turned green and collapsed on his knees.

"Forgive me, my lord, spare me!" he cried, trembling and shaking all over.

"Master Faintheart," said the Prince, articulating each word slowly, "you have been a traitor to your country. In the name of our country, I sentence you to a traitor's death: you are to die by hanging."

"Spare me!" cried the traitor. "*Forgiveness!*"

And pitiful, his face distorted by fear, he rolled himself on the ground at the Prince's feet, seeking to kiss them.

The Prince stood up in disgust.

"It is your country that condemns you," he said.

And turning towards his soldiers, he added gravely:

"Do your duty."

With that, he turned to leave. One of the soldiers cast a rope around the branch of the nearby tree.

"Not here!" said the Prince, pointing at the dead youth. "This is hallowed ground."

The soldiers dragged Master Faintheart to the riverbank, to the roots of a mighty oak.

And before the sun had come out, the traitor had paid for his crime.

XVI

The Belt of Polydorus

T HE SOLDIERS had very little time to rest that day.
The enemy had left, yet there was much to be done.
The master builder with his apprentices secured the bridge
back into place, the soldiers buried the dead, foes and
friends alike, and Miserlix returned to the mine and to the
smithy with his brother, in order to make new arms and in
sufficient numbers so that they might resume the fighting
and drive the enemy far beyond the borders.

The Prince, after setting up his camp and posting guards
all around, sent out scouts to see where his enemies were,
and how many were left. Then he went up the mountain
to the palace.

The windows were flung wide open, and he was greatly
astonished not to hear the usual shrieks of Jealousia and
Spitefulnia. He went straight to the scullery, hoping to see
first Little Irene.

The scullery was neat and tidy. Some wild greens were
simmering gently in a copper pot on the fire, but his sister

was not to be found there, so he went to look for her in the great dining hall.

The door was open.

The King, hands in his pockets, was pacing up and down, pensive and nervous.

The Queen was sitting by the table, striving with infinite perseverance to fashion a crown out of strips of lead foil and odd bits of tin. Only the crown kept breaking up, and the Queen had to start over and over, again and yet again.

Sitting on the window ledge, Little Irene was gazing at the river, and every now and then would wipe her eyes, bright red and swollen from crying.

She got up to go outside, and saw in front of her the Prince, his head bandaged and his arm hanging limp by his side.

She let out a scream, and threw herself at his neck. "Where have you been? What happened to you?" she cried.

The King turned around sharply.

"What's that? Is it you, at last?" he said half-angrily, half-delightedly. "It was about time you remembered to come back to your father's house! Have you no thought to spare for us here, and what we are going through, while you spend all your time gallivanting around the town? Fine things have happened since you left us! Your sisters have gone a-wandering with the maids-in-waiting!"

"Yes, indeed!" added the Queen without getting up, entirely absorbed in her crown. "They left, the heartless girls, and they did not take me with them!"

The Prince stood still, transfixed and dazed.

"And where did they go?" he asked.

"Your guess is as good as mine!" replied the King, gesticulating wildly. "They left without telling us anything, and they took with them what food was left from yesterday, so that today we ourselves have nothing to eat!"

"Yes, we do, father," said Little Irene, wiping her eyes, which kept welling up with tears. "I gathered eggs in the woods and I have boiled wild sorrel. You'll see. I shall make you a lovely sorrel soup…"

"That's it, of course! We shall be living on greens from now on!" said the King. "And not just any greens! Wild greens at that!"

And turning to his son, he said abruptly:

"And as for you, did you at least think of killing a wildfowl or two?"

"No," replied the Prince, "I did not find the time."

"Of course you did not! You run around with strangers, and what strangers! A fine lot of lowlifes, and as for your own, you do not even spare a thought!" said the King.

Changing tone all of a sudden, however, he asked:

"So tell me, what did you do yesterday with all those raving lunatics? And what happened to your head? Was it they who hit you? How did you get rid of them?"

"I did not get rid of them," said the Prince with heartfelt emotion. "I led them into battle, where they fought as lions and were victorious, and they saved your kingdom; and many died, father, so your son might be spared…"

The King stopped, somewhat ashamed on account of all the thoughtless words he had been uttering.

"What's that?! Has there been a battle?" he asked meekly. "But why did you not say so before?"

"And you have been wounded!" cried out Little Irene, struggling to control her sobs.

The Prince recounted to them how the master builder had constructed the bridge; how the soldiers had crossed to the opposite bank under cover of darkness and had taken the sleeping camp by surprise, forcing the enemy to flee, their king with them. He told them with what valour they had fought till daybreak, with farming tools instead of weapons, without food, weary, exhausted, and yet devoted to the end to the Prince who led them.

The King was listening to him, first in astonishment, then with deep-felt emotion, and finally with such enthusiasm that he could no longer control himself, and he clasped his son in his arms.

"You, *it is you who made them worthy!*" he cried. "*You* snapped them out of their stupor; you are the one who deserves to govern them. It is you I shall make king!"

Just at that moment, Polycarpus arrived, too.

"My lord," he said, "the soldiers are hungry! We went to the grocer on the square to get olives and broad beans, only he won't give out anything on credit, he says, not without payment. And no one has any money, since no one worked yesterday. What are we to do?"

The Prince unbuckled a wide leather money belt from around his waist and took out a couple of florins.

"Pay for the broad beans and the olives," he said. "The soldiers are to eat as much as they want. For today this should be enough. As for tomorrow, we will see later what we must do."

The King was in raptures when he saw the florins.

"Where did you find these?" he asked, delighted. "Send Polycarpus at once to buy us a nice fat turkey or two…"

And he reached out to take the money belt. But the Prince stopped his outstretched hand.

"These florins are sacred, father, they have been stained with blood," he said.

And he pointed to a large red blotch, which spread across the money belt.

"Polydorus paid for these with his life," he added with feeling. "They shall be spent, to the last coin, on our country's behalf."

"And how do you intend to spend them?" asked the King, feeling vexed and annoyed. "What more do you need to do? The enemy is gone and dealt with!"

"The enemy is not gone, even if he remains unseen," said the Prince. "And even if he had retreated far beyond the borders, that would not suffice either, for we have no citadels, no army to stop him from coming back."

"And it is with these florins that you hope to build citadels and provide for an army?" asked the King, laughing outright. "But, my boy, you need whole cisterns full of florins to do what you say, and still the money would not suffice."

"I shall start with these," said the Prince, "and before these are spent, perhaps I shall come by some more."

"Where? Just tell me where and how?" asked the King, who was becoming peevish once again.

"Where? How?" said the Prince, considering this carefully. "Perhaps by labouring the land, which will nourish us in turn."

"In a few years then, is that it? And until that time comes, we shall be eating sorrel soup prepared by Little Irene, I presume?"

The Prince lifted up his head.

"Yes, father!" he said resolutely. "For some years the entire land will be eating sorrel soup, and we shall set the example, until the earth can learn to yield its riches once again."

Deep in thought he went down the mountain and headed towards the camp.

That he needed florins he knew well. But where was he to find them?

He looked around him, and dark gloom filled his heart as his gaze fell upon the uncultivated fields, the roads infested with thorns and potholes, and the desolate villages, which had once been inhabited, prosperous and thriving.

He was passing by the woods. He went through the trees, and sat on the grass to rest. Farther down, a streamlet gurgled sweetly, rolling its crystalline waters through the thick undergrowth.

In his mind, the Prince was counting how many more days he could feed his soldiers with Polydorus's florins. And once they had consumed them all, what would they live on, workmen and soldiers alike?

"Oh, if only I had riches! *Great riches!*" he sighed with feeling.

"Well, make them," said a female voice nearby.

"Knowledge!" cried the Prince.

He ran to the thick undergrowth, pushed the branches to the side, and saw Knowledge on her knees, washing clothes in the water of the stream.

"You did not expect to see me here?" she asked, smiling.

"No, your house is so far away! Why do you come here to do the washing?"

"We no longer live in the cottage, which was too close to the river," replied Knowledge. "We left as soon as the enemy had crossed the borders, then came here and hid in the woods together with our cow, our chickens and anything else we were able to carry with us. But tell me now, what is it that distresses you?"

"I have great need of florins, as many as could fill a cistern, and I only have these," said the Prince, pointing to his money belt. "How can I even begin to accomplish the merest trifle with so very little?"

"Begin by buying wheat, barley, broad beans, rice and anything else you could sow," answered Knowledge.

"Have your soldiers cultivate the fields when they are not engaged in fighting. Hire workmen to lay down new roads and build you storehouses, where you will keep your crops, until you can share them out during the winter, when the forest will be covered with snow, and the wild greens will no longer be in season. Moreover—"

"Moreover the forest with its game, the plain with its wild greens, and the river with its fish shall keep us fed," interrupted the Prince, his spirit stirred. "Oh, Knowledge! I shall never be able to repay you for all the good you have done me with the advice that you have given me each time I have met you."

And he dashed off to the camp.

XVII

Work

T HE SCOUTS were coming back just then, bringing the news that the enemy had been disbanded, dispersed and scattered, others here and others there, that the entire plain was bestrewn with the arms they had abandoned in their flight, and that the King the Royal Uncle, as a result of his spite and his rage, had fallen ill, and had summoned from his own country the most learned sage to cure him. He intended, he said, once he was well, to raise a new army and resume the warfare.

The Prince then had some of his people gather the discarded weapons of their enemies. He sent Polycarpus to the capital to buy wheat, barley and anything else that could be sown. He sent others to every corner of the kingdom to purchase oxen from the farmers and also their ploughs, which had stood rusting for countless years in the derelict stables.

And seeing the soldiers sitting with their arms crossed, chatting away the time, or lying basking in the sun, or strolling along the riverbank, he summoned them all together and he said to them:

"Come on, countrymen, let us go and plough the fields, so that when they bring us the wheat, we shall be ready to sow."

And picking up a hoe, he was about to start digging the earth to set the example.

But the soldiers did not let him.

"Not today, my lord," they told him. "You can't, not with your wounded arm and bandaged head! Let us do this work. Just tell us where to begin."

And so, after setting them to work, he took again the road to the capital, and from there he headed for the schoolmaster's house.

As before, he found two or three famished children there, who were watering and raking the garden of the School of the State—while, lounging lazily astride two chairs, his arm resting on a third, was the schoolmaster, reading Xenophon's *Anabasis of Cyrus*.

"Ah, no, this cannot go on any longer!" the Prince said severely. "The time has come for all of us to work, and that includes you, schoolmaster."

The schoolmaster set down his book, and with a hint of sarcasm in his voice, asked:

"What work can I do? As if I could bring the place into order on my own!"

"You and I and all of us, together we shall bring the place into good order, setting first ourselves to rights!" said the Prince angrily.

"And what could I do, for example?"

"Work, instead of sitting here idle and with your arms crossed!"

Very ashamed, the schoolmaster rose from his seat.

"You have work to give me?" he asked.

"As much as you want," replied the Prince. "First of all, take these children here who work in your garden and come with me."

The schoolmaster took the children with him and followed the Prince to Miserlix's smithy, where a great crowd of young boys and girls came and went, carrying iron from the mines to the blacksmith's workshop.

"Good greetings to you, my lord," said Miserlix gaily. "See what good that first street urchin's example has done to the land! The entire capital is sending me now its children, so they might at least earn their bread. And I have no idea how to feed all these people! My stock of grain has almost run out!"

As he spoke, he was still tirelessly striking away with his hammer at the iron on his anvil.

"That's quite all right, Miserlix," said the Prince. "The forest is right at you doorstep, and there are many deer, hares, rabbits and wildfowl, while the plain is filled with wild rocket."

And turning to the children, who were staring at his bandaged head and wounded arm with eyes full of questions:

"Who amongst you knows how to shoot with a sling?"

They all knew. The sling was the only toy they had ever had.

The Prince turned then to the schoolmaster.

"So, then, master scholar, take this down…"

And he dictated the daily schedule, which the schoolmaster wrote down as follows.

Two hours in the morning and two more in the afternoon were to be spent working in the mineshafts; each child was to carry iron back to Miserlix's house. One further hour in the morning and one in the afternoon were to be spent doing lessons; the schoolmaster was to hold the lesson in the woods when the weather was fair, and in the School of the State when the weather was foul. And any remaining hours were to be devoted to hunting.

"Each morning every boy will practise shooting with the bow," ordered the Prince. "In the beginning they will be killing harts and deer, and when they are older they will destroy, should there be need, the enemies of their country."

"Long live our Prince!" exclaimed the children with great excitement.

And all together they ran to kiss his hands, his robes, anything they could get hold of.

"And who is to quarry in the mines?" asked Miserlix. "The piles of leftover stones have been used up, and the children cannot both dig and transport."

"The prisoners will be sent down to the pits," replied the Prince. "Instead of rotting away in prison, let them work for the welfare of the state. Only through work can they become decent human beings again."

Master Miserlix had finished making the rope ladder with the help of one or two carpenters, and the children were now able to go up and down the pits freely.

"And you," said the Prince, smiling to Miserlix's daughter, who had brought him coffee in an iron coffee cup as before, "you and the other young women will be cooking soup for all these people, while the Princess will be cooking it at the camp for the entire army."

And so it began, from the littlest things to the very greatest, the restructuring and the rebirth of the kingdom of the Fatalists.

From the camp of the defeated enemy, the Prince collected the tents and the equipment of war, and distributed these to his soldiers. From the dead enemies he took clothes, and stored them in the palace cellars, so that he could distribute them again to the men in the winter when it turned cold.

Afterwards, he divided his soldiers into four units, in accordance with the trade or craft that they each had known before they became soldiers. The farmers ploughed and sowed the fields; the builders built warehouses and mills and laid out roads; the woodsmen and the carpenters felled trees and worked on the ships of the master builder; and the blacksmiths and the locksmiths worked in the smithy of Miserlix, who oversaw them all.

Every morning, before they applied themselves to any other task, everyone went out hunting, and with their arrows they killed deer, harts, rabbits or wild goats, and with the sling they killed wildfowl, while the elderly, who could no longer rush out to the woods and to the mountains, cast their nets or their lines into the river and caught fish.

Little Irene had come from the palace the moment her brother had spoken to her. Yet when she saw the immense quantities of game and then took one look at her little pots and pans, which would only hold a few small birds at most, she sat down on the grass and burst into tears.

All of a sudden, someone's hand took her own, and a sad voice murmured:

"Do not weep, my Princess, tell me what I may do for you!"

"Oh, Polycarpus!" replied Little Irene. "Where will I stew all the deer and the wild goats that they have brought? I could not even fit one of their heads in my copper pot!"

196

Polycarpus leapt up instantly, ready to dash to the very end of the kingdom to find the cauldron that would be required for the army soup—if this was what it would take to dry his princess's tears.

A sparkling laughter was heard at that moment, however, which made them both start and be still.

Together they turned to look behind them, and saw a girly head smiling at them from between the foliage and the branches.

"The cauldron is right here, Little Irene, bring your game. And you, Polycarpus, come and light the fire for us!" said Knowledge.

They ran to her side, and saw two enormous cauldrons being dragged along by some soldiers. Mistress Wise was leading them, while farther behind came Jealousia and Spitefulnia, smiling and content, as Little Irene had never seen them before. They were carrying between them a large basket filled with wild greens and fruit.

Little Irene was staring at them, stunned with amazement, and it did not even cross her mind to ask how her sisters had come to be there.

Knowledge saw her and started laughing again.

"You did not expect to see your sisters with us, now, did you, Little Irene?" she said. "They got lost in the woods, and grew hungry and tired, so then they remembered the palace, and they wanted to get back. Only they did not know the way. During the night, we heard their crying, and we came out of our tree-hollow, my mother and I. We gave them food, made a bed for them to sleep on, and at earliest dawn all of us together started to work. Because, as you know well, everyone must work in our house."

"But where did you find the cauldrons?" asked Little Irene.

"My mother went and unearthed them from the ruins which used to be the public baths a very long time ago," replied Knowledge. "She thought that those cauldrons, which had been big enough to heat up all that water for the baths, would also be big enough to cook a great quantity of food. Time and rust had eaten away at them, filling them with quite a good number of holes, but Miserlix is an able craftsman, and he patched them easily."

Mistress Wise had set up her cauldrons, Polycarpus had lit the fire, and all the maidens together got busy preparing the army's soup.

Each of them had so much work to do that Jealousia and Spitefulnia quite forgot to quarrel.

"What happened to the maids-in-waiting?" asked Little Irene, when she found herself for a brief instant next to Jealousia, working over the same cauldron.

"Oh! Please! I beg you not to remind me of them!" replied Jealousia with a shiver. "They are the ones who got us all wound up about going away. And when they saw that we had changed our minds, they took all we had and disappeared, abandoning us to our fate."

"And what did you do then?" asked Little Irene with sympathy.

"At first, we began to squabble with each other. One of us would say it was the other's fault. Only, after we had beaten one another viciously, and pulled at each other's hair, and had shed all the tears that we had in our eyes, we decided that it would be better to stop all quarrelling, and seek our way back. So together we came near to where Knowledge was, and it was she who heard our crying and came out to console us and to offer us good shelter."

"Oh, Jealousia!" said Little Irene. "Couldn't you possibly give up quarrelling altogether?"

"All by ourselves, impossible!" said Jealousia. "But Knowledge says she has a special medicine, and that she will give it to us."

"What sort of special medicine?"

"I do not know. Every time I have tried to ask her, she has immediately given me some urgent task to do. And as soon as I finish it, and I go back to ask again, she gives me straight away another task, equally urgent. So that she still has not had a chance to tell me about it. The same with Spitefulnia."

And in the evening, when all the work was done and everyone went to sleep, their weariness was such that the two sisters again forgot to quarrel.

Some days went by in this manner.

The Prince sent out scouts regularly, to find out what the enemies were up to. But the King the Royal Uncle was still so enraged that he could not get better. And his few soldiers who had escaped with their lives from the battle, instead of rallying around him, were going ever farther away, crossing the borders back to their country and returning to their homes.

And so it was that every day the Prince distributed to his soldiers the weapons that Miserlix was making without ever stopping, and he trained them at the bow and the lance. And each day the work of the master builder advanced further, and the ships, from the three that they had been at first, became five, ready to be launched onto the river.

Some weeks went by.

The crops had grown, and the farmers wanted to plant olive trees, pear trees, apple trees, and then they wanted to plant some vegetables. Only there were not enough hands to cultivate all those fields, and those who had sons or daughters abroad began to regret how the country had been emptied of strong hands.

"So why don't you write to your children to come back?" said the Prince to them, for he was never far from their midst.

And those who knew their letters sat down and wrote. And those who did not know how to read or write asked the schoolmaster, who made out for them a letter addressed to their child, or their brother, or their father, and little by little some of those who had left came back, and more weapons and more clothes were needed, and more food.

The Prince went then to the capital and to the villages, and he talked to the women and told them:

"Why are you sitting idle, cooped up in your homes? Your men are at the camp, and working the fields and laying down new roads, building ships, mills and storehouses. Why don't you come too, and help with the preparation of the soup, sew clothes so that your men will have things to wear come winter?"

"And where are we to find the fabric?" the women asked.

"And where are we to find the yarn?"

"You ought to spin the yarn yourselves!"

"Oh, but Prince!" replied the women. "We are but poor folk, we have no sheep. Where shall we find the wool?"

At that, the Prince opened up the precious leather purse of his money belt, and took out a few florins; he then sent Polycarpus together with one or two soldiers to the kingdom of the King the Royal Cousin to buy lambs and sheep.

And when they had brought back the flock, the Prince ordered that they be sheared and that the wool be distributed among the women so they might spin it and weave it and then cut the fabric to make clothes.

He also summoned all the girls and instructed them how to milk the ewes, and under the guidance of Mistress Wise they learnt how to churn butter and make cheese, salt them and store them for the winter when the snows would arrive.

One day, as he was walking through the woods, the Prince saw hanging from a branch an entire beehive, like a big heavy bunch of grapes. He then had the idea of making honey, by assembling together in skeps the bees scattered here and there.

So he took a few big, sturdy reed baskets, and with some soldiers he went around the ravines and the plains and gathered from the tree hollows and the rocks as many bee colonies as he could find, and he brought these back and placed his reed baskets by the entrance of the wood.

And the bees produced so much honey that the Prince decided to harvest it and put it in his storehouses for the winter.

But how was he to get hold of the honeycombs?

"Fumigate the hives with sulphur, my lord," said a lad who had just come back from abroad. "The bees will die, and then you can harvest your honey at your leisure. That's how the Franks do it in their land."

"Why should we kill the bees?" replied the Prince. "It would be quite a shame, now, wouldn't it? We must increase their numbers, on the contrary."

And turning a full skep upside down, he covered it with a large empty basket, and with a few light taps on the outside of the full hive he drove all the bees away and into the empty basket, which he then covered once more, and placed it where the skep had stood previously.

"This is how we can harvest the honey easily, without killing the precious workers who produced it," said the Prince.

He strained the honey into earthenware jars, and he gave the beeswax away, to be melted into thick candles, so they could have light during the winter, when the days would grow short.

202

Several months went by, the crops matured, and the soldiers who were also farmers harvested them and put them in the storehouses built by the soldiers who were also builders.

And everyone who owned a vineyard received an order from the Prince to prune the vine roots neatly and to treat them with sulphur, so they might destroy the aphids that for years now had ravaged the plants, on which the clusters of sour grapes would then rot without ripening.

The soldiers who were also woodsmen had been so industrious that although seven ships were now navigating the river northwards as well as southwards, great stacks of timber still remained, piled up by the riverbanks, and the master builder no longer had the time to use it all, and to drive his nails into the wood.

The Prince saw the heaped logs taking up all this space and it occurred to him that he could find good use for them at once. He had the men load them one day onto three of the ships, and gave orders to Polycarpus to go with some of the soldiers to the nearby kingdom of the King the Royal Cousin.

And while four ships were keeping watch over the river, for the sake of safety, the other three unfurled their sails and set off for the kingdom of the King the Royal Cousin, looking most splendid and majestic.

This monarch was greatly mystified when he was told of this, and he asked to know what was going on with the Fatalists, who were buying sheep and selling timber. Polycarpus merely smiled, however, took the florins, and returned with the three ships to hand the florins to the Prince, who put them overjoyed in the purse of his leather money belt for safe keeping; they were to be used for the upcoming needs of the state.

Thus the winter came, the leaves fell off the trees, the birds flew away to warmer lands, the beasts of the forest hid themselves and the land was covered with snow.

Then the Prince opened up his storehouses, took out the grain, and distributed it to the villagers who carried it to the mills; once ground and milled, they distributed the flour to the women who kneaded it and made bread.

The Prince shared his crops, and so the winter passed and no one had to face hunger.

The children learnt to read and to work, they learnt to shoot arrows and to throw the spear.

XVIII

The King the Royal Cousin

I N THE MEANTIME, however, the King the Royal Uncle had recovered his health.

He sought to reassemble his army, but there was not a single soldier in sight, nor could he track them down any longer.

The blackest melancholy seized hold of him then. He lost his sleep, and he fumed and fretted so much that he could not swallow even a morsel of food.

Seething with rage and tearing at his hair, he crossed the border back into his own land; and once he had regained his capital, he cut off his general's head, because, he claimed, he had deserted the field of battle without requesting permission.

That, however, did little to cure him of his melancholy.

And so he summoned next the humpbacked and bandylegged jester of King Witless, who had found refuge in his palace, having first consumed in feasting and in frolics all the money that he had made for himself by selling the jewels he had stolen from the King of the Fatalists. The King the Royal Uncle commanded the jester to dance before him and to make him laugh.

The jester, however, thanks to the lavish life he had been enjoying, had unlearnt how to dance and how to act the fool; and because of all the rich food that he had been greedily consuming, he was now enormously fat. So that when he tried to dance before his new master, his crooked little legs got into a tangle and he fell panting on the floor.

"What a complete idiot you are!" yelled the King the Royal Uncle in wild frenzy. "You are not even funny any longer! Why should I go on feeding you, vile and ugly as you are?"

And he drew his sword and lopped off the jester's head.

He then summoned his officers; and with terrible threats he ordered them to raise instantly a most fearsome army, cross the border yet again, and lay his nephew's land to waste.

Yet they no longer had any weapons, since the soldiers had abandoned them on the battlefield during their flight. Nor was it so very easy to gather together the men, who had by now scattered to every corner of the kingdom, each of them holed up in his village.

And so it came to pass that, whether he liked it or not, the King the Royal Uncle was forced, for all his seething rage, to postpone his vengeance until a new army might be raised.

The Prince, who was being kept informed of all enemy movements by his secret envoys, ordered a unit of soldiers to leave the camp and proceed all the way to the border, and there erect a mighty citadel, right up on the very top of the rocks, in the exact place where the ruins of the castle built by his grandfather, Prudentius I, could still be seen.

The soldiers carried there provisions for their maintenance; and since the women had gone with them, to knead bread and to cook food, they also had to build some wooden huts to shelter them.

The water, however, seeped in through the cracks between the logs when it rained, and the blustering wind froze them to the bone.

The men therefore decided to build stone cottages, and at nightfall, after their work at the citadel was finished, they would work little by little on their cottage.

And so it came to pass that when it was springtime once again, an entire village had spread at the feet of that great rock, and the Prince ordered them to build a second citadel on the rock next to it, to offer it protection, just at the very spot where there remained the ruins of another old fortress of Prudentius I.

Once some shacks had been erected there as well, the Prince found himself obliged, in order to guarantee their safety, to build a third citadel, and then a fourth, and so on, all along the frontier.

In the meantime, the seven ships had become fifteen, and a good half of these kept sailing away, loaded with timber.

Polycarpus kept coming back with ever more florins, so that they could no longer fit in the purse of the leather money belt, and the Prince had to order a heavy iron coffer with a sturdy lock from Miserlix; he put the florins inside, and kept the coffer under lock and key in the palace cellar.

Knowledge and Mistress Wise did after all accept the Prince's invitation to come up to the palace and live there, for with the very first rain showers, their tree hollow had become uninhabitable.

Together with Knowledge and Mistress Wise, Jealousia and Spitefulnia had also returned to the palace. Since they had been to stay with Knowledge, however, and had shared her work, they had completely unlearnt how to quarrel; and so it happened that when they entered the tower again and saw their rooms with the wrecked furniture strewn everywhere, and the urge came back to them to squabble, they realized all of a sudden that they had forgotten what words to use in order to begin, and they remained for an instant frozen and motionless, staring at one another.

Knowledge, who had only just arrived at that moment herself, sent one of them off to milk the cow, and the other away to weave reed baskets, so they might keep the chickens inside until the henhouse had been rebuilt; and so it came to pass that the two sisters missed their very last chance to resume their old quarrelsome ways.

As a result, tranquillity and soothing silence reigned everywhere in the palace. There was never any screaming to be heard.

The King read his paper in peace every evening, and Knowledge had taught Queen Barmy how to knit stockings; in this way, she managed to win over the King's heart—for he had grown weary, he said, of stepping all day on the bits of broken glass and snippets of tin that the Queen kept scattering everywhere on the floor with all the frills and trinkets she strove to make.

Spring returned, the trees were once again covered with green leaves, the strawberries pushed through, ripening nicely, and the wild rocket grew plentiful everywhere; the birds came back from their wintering places, and hunting was resumed. The farmer-soldiers sowed anew, not only the fields of the previous year, but new ones as well, and agriculture was re-established throughout the realm.

From the camp to the capital, and from there again to the smithy of Miserlix, there was now a long, wide and well-paved road.

The Prince ordered then the woodsmen-soldiers to stop cutting down the trees from the forests along the river, and to begin felling those in the wooded thickets close to Miserlix's smithy. And there, where they had felled many trees, he had them plant young saplings, so that these might grow and be useful at a later time.

With the very last load of timber that the Prince had sent out to be sold to the King the Royal Cousin, the Prince instructed Polycarpus to buy horses, so they could transport the logs more easily to the riverbank.

Together with the horses, he ordered also chickens and ducks, geese and goats. And once the ships returned, he distributed the poultry and the goats to the villages, with the order that each householder should build a pen and a coop. And every day he travelled, now to this village, now to the next, to see whether the villagers were looking after their livestock, and whether they had followed his instructions.

As soon as the village women saw the skilfully built pens and the tidy henhouses, they felt the urge to have each a small garden of their own, where they could grow their vegetables, instead of having to go all the way to the woods every day to collect wild greens.

And next to the garden, they also felt the urge to spruce up their own little cottages. And those whose sons were still abroad had the schoolmaster write them a letter to tell them to come back.

The schoolmaster wrote a letter, which read as follows:

Come back, my child, the good days have returned to our land, everyone has come home, and is earning his bread here today; you alone are still left withering away on your lonesome in foreign parts!

The women were deeply touched when the schoolmaster read this out to them, and each one wanted this letter for her own child, because, as they said, it was so very lovely! The schoolmaster therefore wrote out the same letter for all, and the letters were sent out.

The youths who were still abroad came back to their villages, young Penniless amongst them; seeing everyone else's vineyard green and thriving, he too applied himself to the task of pruning his climbing vine and cultivating his small garden.

After the example of old Penniless, his neighbour too planted a climbing vine. The other neighbours saw this, and they too planted theirs. Those who had pruned and treated their vineyards with sulphur the previous summer had such a bounteous harvest of grapes that they loaded ships, and sent the grapes to be sold in the kingdom of the King the Royal Cousin.

The beehives had multiplied. They collected the honey in earthenware jars, and together with the grapes they had it all sent abroad to be sold.

"What on earth is going on in the kingdom of those Fatalists?" asked once again the King the Royal Cousin. "They buy lambs and horses, for which they pay with golden florins, they sell mountains of timber and grapes and honey. Could it be that the Regent, my cousin, has finally snapped out of his slumber?"

Polycarpus merely smiled, however, as he had done before, and did not speak; he simply took the florins and left with the ships.

His Majesty then sent for his High Chancellor and told him:

"You are to go to the kingdom of the Fatalists, and travel to its every corner. Afterwards you are to come to me and give me a full account of what you did and did not see."

The High Chancellor went; and he toured all the villages and towns. He came back to his king and this is what he said to him:

"I saw a country where all the roads are well laid, and all the houses are neatly built and freshly painted white; I saw villages where all the cottages are well cared for, surrounded by little orchards filled with orange trees, apple trees, cherry trees and other trees and vegetables; I saw field after field sown with wheat and barley, broad beans and corn, stretching farther than the eye can see. And I saw at each dwelling one or two goats, some  chickens, ducks and geese; I saw the prairies swarming with lambs; at evenfall, I saw herds of cows coming down the mountains. I saw smiling faces, and heard singing everywhere. And I did not meet a single beggar."

The King began to pace up and down deep in thought; then he spoke to his High Chancellor.

"What you say is all well and good. But I will not be hoodwinked. The King of the Fatalists has always been a dunce. He never armed a single soldier in his life. How is he to defend all this if ever I were to get the urge to go and take it from him?"

"I saw," the High Chancellor said in turn, "the river packed tight with ships, and I counted amongst them ten or so which were clad all over with iron. Crossing our borders, I saw a citadel on each rock and mountain top, with tremendous turrets. I saw soldiers everywhere I turned to look. I saw small children shooting with the bow, hunting deer and killing birds at the snap of one's fingers!"

"What stuff and nonsense are you telling me?" interjected His Majesty. "You did not dream of these things, by any chance?"

"I saw them with my own eyes, my lord, I touched them with my hands."

"How can this be, then? Did that beggarly cousin of mine stumble across some treasure? Tell me, what does his palace look like?"

"I walked by a mountain bursting with greenery, where, amongst the vegetation, the blossoming orange trees vied with the flowering almond trees for beauty, as lovely in their attire as brides on their wedding day. I went all the way up and was greatly astonished to find there a great half-ruined edifice, with a donjon tower, which alone seemed habitable. At the windows, I saw spotless white curtains, and all around the tower there were cows and goats grazing, keeping good company with the chickens. Passing under an open window, I heard sparkling female laughter. But I saw no one. I descended the mountain, and asked who lived in that ruin. And the people answered: 'The King!' I did not believe them, so I asked elsewhere. Again they told me that it was the King's palace. And again I did not believe them, and I went to the camp, which is by the river. There I saw many tents, but few soldiers, so I asked where the men were. They replied: 'In the fields!' And I asked who lived in the ruin on the summit of the mountain. And again they said: 'The King!' Seeing my bafflement, they indicated a youth who was just arriving, dressed in white woollen clothes, same as all the other soldiers, his arrows in a quiver slung behind his back, bow in hand. His face was covered with dust and dripping with sweat; around his waist he wore an old leather money belt, where a large dark stain could be seen. All the soldiers ran to him, and kissed his hands as soon as they saw him. And such was the joy that spread over their faces that I found myself bewildered, and I asked who it was. And they replied: 'The Prince!' Again, I did not believe them, and I laughed and asked them: 'He wouldn't also be living up there in the ruin on the mountain top, would he?' And they answered: 'No. That is where his father lives, the King. The Prince lives here with us.' Then I left, my lord, and came back to tell you what I had seen and heard."

For a brief moment, the King the Royal Cousin remained speechless. Then very slowly, as though a great truth had been revealed to him, he said:

"Prudentius has risen from the grave!"

And he commanded that they bring to him from his treasuries a golden crown, bedecked with precious emeralds and diamonds, which his father had won as his trophy in a great battle, after killing with his own hand the king who had worn it. He placed it in a beautifully wrought silver casket, sealed it, and handed it to the High Chancellor.

"Take with you immediately fifty of my best guardsmen and go with them to the Prince of the Fatalists, to whom you are to present this crown together with my swift-footed, snow-white mare; you are to ask him to accept the gifts I send him, the most precious possessions that I have in my treasuries, and to tell him that I seek his alliance and his friendship. Go now!"

XIX

The King the Royal Uncle

I N THE MEANTIME, the King the Royal Uncle, after having toiled and struggled for three years, had managed to raise sufficient armed forces to relaunch his war campaign against his nephew, the King of the Fatalists.

He mounted his best steed, he belted on his great sword; his trumpeters were positioned at the forefront, proclaiming their progress through the land with a triumphant military march.

"Onwards, lads," he cried out to his soldiers. "We shall stroll our way unopposed straight into the palace of the Regent himself."

They walked for some few hours.

Gazing at the prairies across which he had retreated vanquished and dishonoured three years earlier, the King the Royal Uncle reckoned that this time, on his intended glorious return, he would be dragging behind him King Witless and the Prince, tied with ropes from the saddle of his horse. And he laughed a satanic laugh, and rejoiced in advance at the shame and tears of his nephews.

"Oh! You shall pay so very dearly for that one victory of yours!" he grunted, menacing the open horizon with his fist.

All of a sudden, however, he stopped short, rubbed his eyes. Then he looked ahead once more, then to the right, after that to the left, pinched his arm hard to see whether he might mayhap be dreaming in his sleep, then rubbed his eyes hard a second time.

"But what has come over me, then?" he said uneasily. "Am I dreaming wide awake?"

He thundered:

"*General!*"

The General approached and bowed to the ground.

"Your Majesty?"

"Look ahead and tell me, what do you see?"

"A citadel, Your Majesty."

"You are as blind as a mole! Summon the Major-General!" said the King crossly.

The Major-General came and bowed to the ground.

"Your Majesty?"

"Take a look around you, there, towards the border, and tell me, what can you see?"

"Citadels, Your Majesty."

"You are an ass!" yelled the King the Royal Uncle wildly. "An ass and a traitor! Order the Centurion to come here at once, and vanish from my sight!"

The Centurion too came, and bowed to the ground.

"Can you make out that mountain over there?" the King the Royal Uncle asked curtly.

"Yes, Your Majesty."

"What is that thing on top of it, a pile of rubble or something of that sort?"

"It is not rubble," said the Centurion, shading his eyes with his hand, "it is a mighty citadel—"

He had no time to finish. With a sweep of his sword, the King the Royal Uncle had lopped off his head.

Then he turned to his soldiers and shouted to them, foaming with rage:

"What is perched up there, lads, will someone finally tell me?"

And the whole army in one voice cried out:

"A citadel, and farther down another citadel, and farther down another citadel; as far as the eye can see, citadels and more citadels!"

Then the King the Royal Uncle hung his head low on his chest and cried with blind fury.

He sent a reconnaissance party ahead, to see what all these citadels were like. But as soon as the scouts even tried to get nearer, a storm blast of arrows greeted them and drove them to mad flight.

They went farther away, everywhere was the same.

They attempted to pass between two citadels, and from both sides so many arrows flew out at them that half the soldiers were left dead on the spot.

As soon as the King the Royal Uncle saw that he could no longer get through, he bit his hands with such rage, and he filled up inside with so much yellow bile, that he was taken ill again and had to return to his palace.

He remained there for some days, brooding with spite, holed up in his rooms. Then he summoned his High Chancellor and said to him:

"Take immediately ten of the best soldiers in my personal guard, go to the kingdom of the Fatalists and tell the Prince to come to me at once, for I wish to give him in marriage the hand of the Princess, my royal daughter. Go now!"

The High Chancellor left with the ten bodyguards, and went to the kingdom of the Fatalists, where he requested to see the Prince.

They led him to a tent. Sitting on a wooden stool, before a roughly fashioned wooden table, a youth was reading some sheets of paper. From the corner of his eye, the High Chancellor saw with bewilderment that these sheets of paper bore the golden seal of the King the Royal Cousin.

The youth wore white woollen clothes, and differed in nothing from the other soldiers who surrounded him, except for a shabby leather money belt that he wore around his waist; a black stain could be seen spreading across it.

And yet kneeling in front of this youth was an elderly nobleman, richly attired in gold-embroidered robes of velvet, holding a precious silver casket in his hands. With profound respect he was waiting for the youth to finish his reading so he could then present the casket to him.

The young man lifted up his head, and saw the envoy of the King the Royal Uncle.

"Who are you and what is your purpose?" he asked.

"I seek audience with the Prince, the son of the King of the Fatalists," replied the High Chancellor.

"I am he," said the Prince. "Now, state your business."

For all that he was so very simply dressed, there was such nobility in his voice and in the way he carried himself that the envoy of the King the Royal Uncle fell on his knees.

"Your Royal Highness!" he said. "The King your Royal Uncle and my liege has commissioned me hither to bid you come to his kingdom at once, for he wants you to marry his daughter the Princess."

The Prince's eyes flashed, but he restrained himself.

"Tell your lord that I do not take orders from him. I shall not come as he bids. But I would not like you to leave empty-handed. Your master offered a gift once to my father, the King. Then we were not in a position to return his generosity in kind. But now I shall give you to take to your liege a gift worthy of the honour he conveys upon me by choosing me among all other men to be his son-in-law and husband of his daughter the Princess."

He motioned to Polycarpus, who left that very instant, leapt on his horse, and galloping flew up to the palace, where he dismounted and rushed into the dining hall.

The King was playing a game of chess with Mistress Wise. Sitting by the window, Jealousia was singing and turning her spinning wheel, while next to her, silent and smiling, Spitefulnia was stuffing a pillow.

Sunk in deep concentration, Knowledge and Little Irene were examining at the table the records of the cook's expenses; Queen Barmy was knitting a woolly hat for the old King's bald head.

Polycarpus dashed straight up to Little Irene.

"My Princess, the donkey's head! The hour has come!" he cried, his voice faltering.

Nobody understood him.

"What hour? What are you talking about?" they all asked.

Little Irene alone understood. She stood up, blushing with delight.

"Has a message come from the King the Royal Uncle?" she asked.

"Yes, my Princess," replied Polycarpus. "He is seeking to have the Prince as his son-in-law."

"What's that?" bellowed the King.

Knowledge had risen too, and asked nervously:

"What answer did the Prince give?"

"Here is his answer!" cried Little Irene happily.

And climbing on a stool, she seized from above the gold-leaf cabinet the donkey's head that hung there on a nail with its tin crown; she wrapped these in the red silk scarf that she had kept safely away in her drawer, and put everything in a basket. Then she sewed a sturdy piece of canvas over the top, and handed the basket to Polycarpus.

The equerry mounted his horse once more, and galloped down to the camp.

The Prince took the basket, and handed it to the envoy of the King the Royal Uncle.

"Take this," he said, "and give it to your liege. Do not forget to repeat to him the words I said to you. Now go."

And turning to the High Chancellor of the King the Royal Cousin, he said:

"Tell your lord that I thank him. Gifts my father the King cannot send him yet, for our kingdom is still poor, and we need all our florins. But our friendship he will indeed have, and joyfully we accept his offer of alliance, which does us honour. Godspeed to you."

The two envoys bowed deeply, and each went on his way.

XX

Prudentius II

SILVER CASKET IN HAND, the Prince leapt on the white mare, the gift of the King the Royal Cousin, and accompanied by Polycarpus he scaled the mountain all the way up to the palace.

The table was already set. They were waiting for the two of them before they might begin.

The Prince ran up to his father, knelt before him and handed him the silver casket.

"My father and my king," he said with feeling, "I took away from you your crown one day, when the nation demanded sacrifices from each of us. Today the nation lifts up its head once more, it has become strong, and with its strength it now inspires the respect of its enemies. Take back your crown, my king and father, it is the nation's gift to you."

The King lifted up the lid, and, seeing the magnificent crown with its precious stones, he stood there stunned, his mouth agape.

"What is this? How came you by it?" he asked at last.

"It is the gift of the King our Royal Cousin, who asks for our friendship and desires an alliance with us," replied the Prince.

The King then rose, took the crown from the casket, and placed it on his son's head.

"You wear it, my son," he said, visibly moved. "You deserve such a crown, because it is with your hard efforts and your strength that you have succeeded in earning it. A while ago now, I made you Regent and my equal. Now I am an old man, I am weary of hearing about matters that require my attention; I wish to spend my final years in peace. You take the crown, together with its heavy burdens, and rule now on your own the kingdom you have raised from the dead by force of will alone."

The following day, the King convened all his people to the camp by the riverbank, and there announced to everyone that he was stepping down from his position as ruler of the State, and that he was surrendering the crown and the kingship to his son, the Prince.

With these words, he placed the precious crown on his son's head, and anointed him King of the Fatalists.

From every breast, there sprang a great cry:

"Long live Prudentius II! Long live our King!"

The people's joy knew no bounds. They all wanted to kiss the hands of the old King who had recognized the worth of his son, and of the new King, the saviour of their nation.

That day was proclaimed a holiday across the entire land.

When the new king, Prudentius II, went up to the palace with his new High Chancellor, Polycarpus, he found again all the family gathered in the dining hall.

He looked at the empty hook on the wall above the gold-leaf cabinet, and let a deep sigh escape from his lips.

"Now that that revolting donkey's head is gone," he said, "I can finally say that I feel free to undertake great things."

And, turning to Knowledge, who was smiling at him, joyful and blushing pink:

"Would you like to help me, Knowledge?"

"I?" exclaimed the maiden, turning an even deeper hue of scarlet. "I? How could I be of help to you?"

"Be my wife and my queen," said Prudentius. "You have done me so much good with your advice! Tell me, Knowledge, wouldn't you like to help me govern this land?"

But before the maiden had time to reply, the old King had clasped both of them in his arms.

"With all my blessings," he said, "*yes! Together* you shall rule the state."

"And when the King our Royal Uncle finds out about your engagement, what will he say?" asked Little Irene, laughing gaily.

"He shall request your hand for his son," said Mistress Wise. And with a wink made a sign to the King to look at Polycarpus.

The miserable High Chancellor had grown ashen upon hearing the words of Mistress Wise; trembling all over, he too was looking at Little Irene, as though expecting to hear from her lips his own death sentence.

The Princess blushed a bright ruby red, turned and saw him; she lowered her eyes, shy and numb.

"And… would you accept that offer, my Princess?" asked the High Chancellor, his voice choking.

"No, Polycarpus…" murmured Little Irene, without looking at him.

"I do indeed hope that the King our Royal Uncle shall never extend to us such an offer," said Prudentius, laughing mirthfully. "Or his anger will have reason to flare up again. For we very much desire Little Irene to remain here."

And taking his sister's hand, he placed it on the hand of Polycarpus, who almost lost his wits for joy.

"On the contrary! He should make the offer, so that he might receive a second serving of our contempt!" said the old King, who could still not put the donkey's head out of his mind.

And happy, embracing his children, he added:

"And should the whimsy take him, just let him come back with his army and then he shall feel indeed how sharply Miserlix's arrows can pierce."

But the poor King the Royal Uncle never had a chance of receiving that second mighty serving of contempt, nor did he have occasion to test whether Miserlix's arrows could pierce or not.

When he opened the basket and recognized the donkey's head, and heard the Prince's words as repeated to him by his High Chancellor, such mad fury seized hold of him that he fell like a log on the floor.

And when they lifted him up to carry him to his bed, they saw that he was dead.

On the day of his coronation, Prudentius II went to the river to hold a memorial service in honour of all those who had fallen during that famous nocturnal battle.

Under the shade of the plane trees, two white crosses stood side by side: the grave of Polydorus and the grave of the youth from the tavern.

Prudentius placed a laurel wreath on each cross.

"Place a second wreath on this one, my lord," said the master builder, indicating Polydorus's grave.

"A second wreath? What do you mean?"

"In honour of the Unrevealed Hero," replied the master builder.

Prudentius cast him a hard look.

"I do not understand," he said.

"The one-armed man never made it back from his last crossing," my lord.

"What became of him, do you know? Have you had any news?" asked Prudentius.

The master builder slowly shook his head.

"For three years now I have waited for him," he said, "and every nightfall, once the sun has set, I have come back to this same place, in the hope that perhaps he would return. But now I no longer expect him to come back…"

"He may have gone abroad, like so many others," said Prudentius.

The master builder considered this carefully.

"I know that he did not," he said at last. "As I knew him, he was a man who would have given up his life without many words, silent and unrevealed, for the sake of his country. Abandon his homeland during a time of danger? That he would never have done!"

For a good while neither of the two spoke.

Then the new King cut a laurel branch from the tree and laid it on Polydorus's grave.

"To the Unrevealed Hero…" he said.

"And to all those who give up their lives in silence and with humility for the sake of their country, without their homeland ever coming to know who they were…" added the master builder.

And kneeling, they both paid their homage before the grave.

THE END

PUSHKIN PRESS

Pushkin Press was founded in 1997. Having first rediscovered European classics of the twentieth century, Pushkin now publishes novels, essays, memoirs, children's books, and everything from timeless classics to the urgent and contemporary.

This book is part of the Pushkin Collection of paperbacks, designed to be as satisfying as possible to hold and to enjoy. It is typeset in Monotype Baskerville, based on the transitional English serif typeface designed in the mid-eighteenth century by John Baskerville. It was litho-printed on Munken Premium White Paper and notch-bound by the independently owned printer TJ International in Padstow, Cornwall. The cover, with French flaps, was printed on Colorplan Pristine White paper. The paper and cover board are both acid-free and Forest Stewardship Council (FSC) certified.

Pushkin Press publishes the best writing from around the world—great stories, beautifully produced, to be read and read again.